VIOLA THE GREAT

© Troy Harwood-Jones

20251102

ISBN: 978-1-0697068-8-1

www.harwoodjones.com

The Known World
Hoss Haus Sea
WEST HOSS
EAST HAUS
Mouth of Doom
Iambic Sea
FAE ISLES
Sea of Flumes
HERE BE MOISTURE
BOLVO
MOLGOROD
CRACKENDOR
THE HIGH REPUBLIC MORELESS
ONJON

Chapter 1

The kingdom of Dampenia was a small, very soggy country tucked between two enormous lands that enjoyed breaking things. Honestly, it was surprising Dampenia existed at all. Mostly, it survived through a lucky mix of bad weather and worse maps. Marching armies sank into puddles that seemed to have no end. Mapmakers simply left a damp smudge and wrote: *Here Be Moisture.*

Inside that smudge, the Dampenian people lived as happily as wet allows—making umbrellas, weaving towels, and pretending this was perfectly ordinary. Which, for them, it was.

Dampenians were the sort of folk who accepted what life gave them and didn't complain. Each morning the town crier climbed the public stairs—slowly, so he wouldn't slip—and announced the forecast.

"Good citizens! Merwin, the royal weather wizard, predicts light rain followed by an easterly drizzle. Tonight: heavy showers—or sleet, if we are unlucky!"

Everyone nodded politely under their umbrellas. They always nodded, even though Merwin was almost always wrong.

To be fair, weather magic was tricky work. And whether it rained before or after it drizzled, the result was much the same: wet.

At the centre of this perpetually damp realm stood the capital, Dropminster. A wall circled the city, and beyond it lay a moat—kept more out of habit than defence. In its heart rose the royal castle, built of white stone—which was, perhaps, not the best idea. White shows stains. But Queen Drizzila had always dreamed of a bright palace, and King Darius wanted her happy, so the result was now best described as white-ish. The royal gardener, who took such things personally, had covered the castle in climbing vines. By midsummer it looked like a giant bouquet that had fallen into the city and decided to stay.

And into this wet, shining city came Viola—our hero, though no one knew that yet.

Viola was, by general agreement, unusual. She was always cheerful, and nothing seemed to fix it. In the gloom of Dampenia, she shone like a small, unlicensed ray of sunshine. Most people carried umbrellas; Viola often did not. She liked to skip through puddles, letting her shoes squelch like happy frogs. They were not boots. She had owned several pairs, all lost to causes never clearly explained. Her

mother refused to buy
more, and Viola claimed
she liked the sound her
feet made anyway.

Here she comes now,
tripping along the
cobblestones, singing a
tune known only to
herself. It changed shape
as she went—sometimes
bright, sometimes sad—
but always certain that it
existed. When the song

ran out, she tilted her head, listened to the drizzle, and
found more of it.

Viola also worked. This was odd, since she was only
thirteen and technically too young. But Dampenia was
never a place to let small rules get in the way of useful
work. Through a few mix-ups (all perfectly ordinary),
she had found herself employed at Brennick's Mop
Emporium, which promised "a mop for every
occasion, including most emergencies."

The job opened when the last cleaner quit, claiming
she could no longer mop the mop aisle. "There are
just too many mops," the girl said—which was
accurate but unhelpful. Mr. Brennick, the owner, was
trying to reason with her when Viola walked by,
dripping slightly.

"Maybe I could help," she said.

That was that. The other girl left. Viola stayed.

Her days were long. There was, it turned out, quite a lot to learn about mops—at least according to Mr. Brennick, who had devoted his life to them. But he seemed pleased that Viola hadn't complained about mops being in a mop store, which felt like progress. And Viola liked to be useful. Mops were important. Especially in Dampenia.

She was on her way home one evening when she stopped to splash in a particularly deep puddle, and something floated past her foot.

Something woolly.

A sheep was swimming upstream. But that wasn't what caught her attention. A large, lumpy creature was chasing it. It had wide shoulders, long muddy arms, and was roughly the size of a very hungry wardrobe. It gave a happy howl, tripped over a cabbage cart, and splashed onward. It didn't see Viola and nearly ran her over.

"That's a boggart," muttered Baorick the baker from under his awning. "Third one today."

Viola blinked. "What's it doing in town?"

"Causing trouble," he said. "And eating our sheep."

The boggart caught the sheep and swallowed it in three gulps. Then it burped proudly, jumped over a hedge, and vanished into the mist. A faint splash followed.

"That's not good," said Viola.

"Can't say it is," Baorick agreed. "He didn't even pay for it."

Chapter 2

ne morning, the citizens of Dropminster discovered that the moat was no longer just a moat—it was *inhabited*. A tribe of boggarts had moved in.

Boggarts are large, green-grey humanoids with three fingers and a thumb, four toes, and an alarming number of teeth arranged mostly at random. They stand ten to fifteen feet tall at their prime, though posture is not their strength. Ill-mannered, undressed, and perpetually muddy, they lurch through life helping themselves to whatever catches their fancy—usually edible things like sheep, small dogs, and the occasional unattended picnic. They prefer wet places—bogs, swamps, ditches, and, as it turned out, moats.

Now, boggarts were not unheard of in Dampenia, but these ones were *foreigners*: refugees from the western kingdom of Crackendor, a realm famous for three pursuits—shattering monuments, hosting noisy festivals, and breaking things in the name of national unity.

Crackendor's latest crisis began when someone broke a sacred statue of Someone Important, leading to an argument, a riot, and the usual solution: violent upheaval. The boggarts, finding themselves on the losing side of the argument (and possibly the statue), fled eastward in search of peace and snacks.

Upon reaching Dropminster, they beheld the royal moat and decided it was a vacant residence. By dawn, the city awoke to find boggarts wallowing contentedly in the water, coating themselves in fresh mud, and passing the time with loud belching contests. From time to time, one would reach out and remove a plump sheep from the surrounding pasture for light refreshment.

Still, the Dampenian response was—as ever— resigned.

"Well," they said, "at least they're in the moat and not the bakery."

At Brennick's Mop Emporium, the boggart question was the topic of the morning. Viola was arranging mops by handle length when the first customer, a stout woman in a dripping shawl, began her complaint.

"I'm telling you, Brennick, they're everywhere. The smell alone is enough to curdle a sheep."

"Not good for business," said Mr. Brennick, who believed this about nearly everything.

"They're eating the sheep," the woman continued, "and not *paying* for them. Now there's a shortage of sheep soup."

This caused a small gasp from the line behind her.

Another customer sniffed. "The King should do something about it."

There was a long pause while everyone silently agreed that this was true—and equally unlikely.

Eventually, everyone agreed that things were dreadful but probably not worse than last year. They each bought an extra mop—partly out of habit, partly to feel industrious, and left the shop comforted by the knowledge that nothing would change.

By the time Viola made her way home, the drizzle had indeed turned to sleet, just as the wizard had predicted for once. Their little cottage sat in the east quarter of town, tucked near the old stone walls. It was a modest place: one bedroom she and her mother shared, a little kitchen just big enough for a wooden table and two chairs, and a stove that was almost always slightly damp but usually stocked with enough wood. Moss clung to the stones, and the roof pinged softly with the steady patter of rain. It was cozy, provided you had a taste for perpetual dampness.

Viola hung up her hat and scarf and called cheerfully, "Mum, I'm home!"

Her mother turned from the stove with a smile.

"Oh, that's wonderful, dear. How was your day at Brennick's?"

Viola bubbled on about the endless rows of mops and the sheer number of them—"At least a hundred, Mum!"—while her mother nodded politely, not particularly interested but doing a fine job of pretending.

Her mother had never quite understood Viola's unending enthusiasm. She loved her daughter dearly—fiercely, even—but found her optimism peculiar. Regular folk did not find enjoyment in the world; they endured it. They didn't hum ditties to the rain. They walked through it methodically, umbrella up, collar high, and head down. Still, Viola was her daughter, and love—thankfully—was unconditional.

Eventually, hunger defeated even her prattle, and Viola's thoughts turned to food.

"What's for dinner?" she asked.

"Lamb stew, dear."

Viola beamed. "Oh, I love lamb stew!"

But when she peeked into the pot, lifting the lid and taking a whiff, she saw only potatoes bobbing in a thin, greyish broth, several pricklepeppers, and maybe a bit of tomato—no lamb in sight.

"Mum, I don't see any lamb here," she said.

"Why yes," her mother replied with a shrug, "the boggarts got to it first. You know how it is. The prices went up. So, it's lamb -less lamb stew tonight."

Viola had to admit that made sense, so she simply nodded, accepting it with a little grin.

"I guess it's still soup!"

Mum patted her shoulder. "Better than nothing. Add a little extra pepper, dear, and enjoy."

And they did.

Chapter 3

o everyone's surprise, King Darius did, in fact, attempt to do something about the boggart problem. This was not typical royal behaviour, but Queen Drizzila had reached the end of her tolerance—and her nose.

Unfortunately for the Queen, the Crackendorian boggarts had settled on the western stretch of the city moat—the part directly upwind from her floral bedroom balcony. As a result, each morning she awoke to what she described as "a strong rural perfume with notes of cabbage and despair."

The matter could no longer be ignored.

And so, one damp afternoon, King Darius himself emerged from the vine-covered castle, accompanied by several of his knights. They ascended the western wall, leaned cautiously over the battlements, and looked down at the moat below.

The boggarts were easy to spot. A dozen or so were floating happily in the murky water, singing tunelessly and occasionally dunking each other for sport.

King Darius cupped his hands around his mouth.

"Good morning, er—citizens of the moat!" he called.

The singing stopped. Several boggarts blinked up at him, puzzled. One of them waved what might once have been a flag—or possibly a towel.

"I should like to speak to your leader," the King continued.

This caused a long, thoughtful silence among the boggarts. They did not, as a rule, *have* leaders. After a bit of splashing and argument, the oldest (and largest) among them—identified by the number of barnacles on his shoulders—sloshed to the edge of the moat.

"I'm Grog," he announced. "What do you want?"

King Darius cleared his throat in what he hoped was a regal manner.

"Grog, would you and your people consider relocating—ideally to somewhere else? Our kingdom, as you might have noticed, is very small and not truly the sort of place for large, impressive creatures such as yourselves. May I suggest," and here he smiled as winningly as possible, "that Molgorod is very, ah, charming this time of year? It's only about fifty miles that way," he said, pointing east.

This was, of course, a lie. Molgorod was indeed fifty miles to the east, but it was never charming at any time of year.

If Crackendor, to the west, was the realm of smashing, shouting, and sudden explosions of civic enthusiasm, then Molgorod, to the east, was the opposite sort of disaster—quiet, organized, and utterly humourless.

Where Crackendor's armies marched for glory, Molgorod's marched for order. Its citizens were born wearing uniforms, and many never got around to taking them off. Most were engineers of some sort. The capital, Molgorosk, was a city of perfect squares. Buildings were cubes, often without windows, and occasionally without doors. The streets ran in straight lines from horizon to horizon, which made navigation simple but despair inevitable.

Czar Vortan the Most Efficient hated anything disorderly. Most of the time, he sent strongly worded letters to other nations explaining how they could be more productive. Occasionally, he sent his legions to enforce this advice—either by destroying anything playful or, alternately, by planting his neighbours' crops *properly*, since it was painful to watch someone harvest five bushels of apples when ten could be achieved through improved planning.

Unfortunately for King Darius, these particular refugee boggarts had originally come *from* Molgorod (before fleeing to Crackendor), and so the lie failed immediately.

Grog scratched his chin. "Don't like grids."

Having been stymied, the King tried again.

"Very well. Perhaps you and your, ah, people would be happier on the eastern side of the moat, where the air is fresher?"

The boggart thought about this for a long time, scratching his chin with one oversized finger. Behind him, several others nodded as if in deep consultation, though it was unclear anyone was listening.

Finally, Grog said, "No."

The King blinked. "No?"

"No," Grog repeated, with great satisfaction. Then he added, "We like it here. Smells like home."

King Darius looked at his knights. His knights looked at each other. After a brief silence, the King sighed, adjusted his crown, and announced that negotiations had concluded.

He retreated back into the castle to write a royal decree on *further study of the boggart situation,* which everyone agreed was precisely the sort of action a responsible monarch would take before doing nothing at all.

Chapter 4

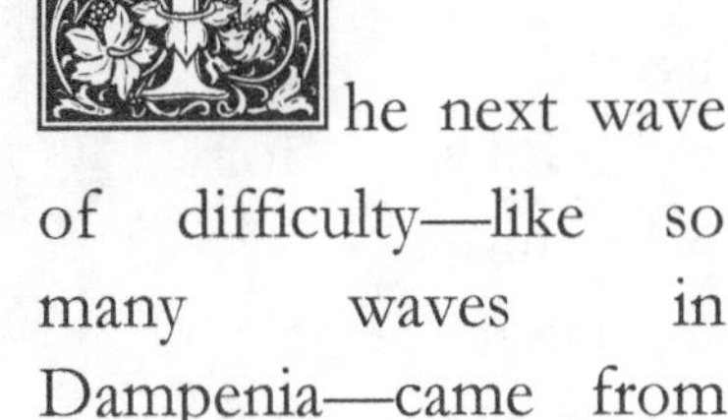he next wave of difficulty—like so many waves in Dampenia—came from the sea.

It began when the Kingdom of Crackendor decided to conquer the Fae Isles: a scattered collection of small, misty islands north of their coast, where the Iambic Ocean meets the Sea of Flumes. On maps, the isles looked like a neat row of stepping stones leading westward toward the distant nation of West Hoss.

No one in their right mind would attempt to use them as actual stepping stones; the waters between were deep, cold, and occasionally missing. But Crackendor was not famous for its right mind. It was generally assumed the conquest had something to do with a new national holiday—or possibly the testing of an experimental war machine large enough to need islands for feet. Whatever the reason, the Fae Isles were declared conquered, saluted, and promptly forgotten.

Unfortunately, the isles were not uninhabited.

They had long
been home to a
population of Fae
merfolk, who had
lived there
peacefully for
generations—
lounging on the
rocks, combing
their hair, and
singing long songs

about how difficult it was to get seaweed out of one's scales. When the Crackendorians arrived with drums and banners and a complete disregard for marine tenancy, the merfolk were driven out in great, slippery crowds.

Before anyone in Dampenia quite knew how, Fae began turning up along its shores—and eventually in its rivers, fountains, and canals. They were hard to miss: tall, shimmering, and mildly offended by everything. On land, they wrapped their tails in damp cloth to keep from drying out and travelled in small, noisy bands, trailing the smell of brine and misfortune. They called themselves the "tide-folk." Most Dampenians called them "the new problem."

Also, the Fae washed their laundry in public fountains.

Also, they sang at all hours.

Also, merfolk don't recognize private property.

It's not part of their culture. Merfolk rarely say "this is mine" about anything not physically attached to them—and have been known to give away things that *are* attached, if the price is right. Unfortunately for the Dampenians, they *do* believe in private property. So, when they came home to find a merfolk living in their house, or sleeping in their bed, or drinking soup from their good bowl, they were not pleased.

Still, the Dampenian response was—as usual—resigned.

"Well," said the citizens, "at least they're not in the moat."

The Queen's royal entourage, however, was less impressed. The merfolk's songs were haunting and beautiful, but mostly about how they'd been wronged. And while tragic ballads were indeed the most popular kind of music in Dampenia, the Fae tended to sing about ongoing wrongs—with choruses about vengeance, revolution, and flaying one's oppressors. Dampenian taste leaned more toward resigned suffering and tragic acceptance. The Fae music felt like a call to battle, which was considered rude.

In desperation, the Queen's musicians challenged the Fae to a battle of the bands—loser to leave the country, winner to be chosen by royal vote.

The Fae were not fooled. They didn't show up.

Now, a little-known fact about the merfolk: they absolutely adore fish. Not to befriend—to eat. It might seem peculiar. After all, these were aquatic folk;

some even had gills. You'd think fish were practically cousins. But fish was their favourite food, and with merfolk now swimming upriver and wandering the countryside, they made short work of the local supply.

Fishermen were disgruntled.

Grocers complained there wasn't a herring or trout to be found.

But in true Dampenian fashion, everyone just sighed and carried on. What could you do?

At Brennick's Mop Emporium, where Viola spent her days organizing endless rows of mops, the customers came in grumbling. No fish stew. No fish broth. No fish bouillabaisse. Viola listened and nodded sagely, trying to mimic Mr. Brennick's supportive demeanour. Everyone was just making do.

That evening, Viola walked home through the drizzle—still humming a little merfolk tune she'd heard in the lane—and found her mother at the table.

"Oh, how was your day?" her mother asked.

"Lovely, Mum. Except everyone's talking about the fish shortage."

"Ah yes," her mother said, "well, as it happens, we're having fish soup tonight."

But of course, when Viola lifted the lid, it was fish soup in name only: a thin broth, a bit of seasoning, and a faint memory of haddock, if you sniffed hard enough.

"Mum... did you buy any fish?"

"Oh no, dear," said her mother. "Too expensive, you know. Fish soup without fish for us tonight." She smiled ruefully and added, "Just add a little extra pricklepepper."

And so she did.

And while it couldn't really be called fish soup, it was still tasty, thanks to the peppers.

Chapter 5

It was, by all accounts, the final straw.

Technically speaking, it wasn't a straw at all, but a blight. Well—one shouldn't get too dramatic about these things. It wasn't even really a blight. It was a swarm.

A swarm of Brean locusts.

Now, the Breans were not ordinary insects. They were a fully developed race of very small, very intelligent, and exceedingly energetic creatures. Endlessly in motion, they spent their days skipping, hopping on the spot, performing box jumps, and exchanging fitness tips and the latest diet advice. Their diets, however, never amounted to much. They would rise at dawn vowing to eat only legumes, and by noon—perhaps owing to all that exercise—be seized by sudden, uncontrollable hunger and devour everything in sight, and a few things just beyond it.

They didn't speak Common, either. They spoke Locus: a complex language of high-pitched leg-rubbing that was inaudible to most civilized ears but deeply upsetting to dogs.

This was, as it turned out, a serious problem for Molgorod.

The Molgorodians valued their dogs. Every household was required—by law—to own at least one Doberman. They were perfectly trained, perfectly silent, and perfectly obedient. They sat in perfect lines, waiting patiently for commands like "attack," "fetch," or "roll over efficiently."

Then came the Breans.

The Breans never stopped chattering. Their noise made every Doberman in the country start barking. Soon, whole towns were shaking with the sound. After a few days, the city of Molgorosk was a loud, barking mess.

Czar Vortan the Most Efficient called it a national emergency. He issued *Order 999: For the Restoration of Calm Dogs.*

In simpler words, it meant: get rid of the Breans.

The Breans, being small, quick, and used to trouble, ran away at once. And because

Dampenia was nearby—and not very well protected—they all fled there. Millions of them.

The Dampenians were kind people. They thought killing a whole species was wrong. But kindness has limits. Before long, their little rainy country was overrun with talkative fitness fanatics—tiny voices everywhere shouting, comparing step counts, and praising the virtues of leaf-based protein—which, not speaking Locus, no one understood. Though quite a few felt vaguely like they should probably get out for a run more often.

Then the Breans began to eat.

They ate almost everything: wheat, barley, carrots, cabbages. But what they loved most—their favourite food in all the world—was anything spicy. Hot peppers. Chili plants. And worst of all, Dampenia's own treasure: pricklepepper.

They ate the peppers first. Then the flowers. Then the leaves, the stems, and finally the roots, working with the efficiency of a species that had opinions about proper deconstruction methodology.

Within a month, the pricklepepper harvest was gone. Within two, so were the plants.

All in all, it was a bad year. But one shouldn't complain.

When things go poorly, the Dampenians go shopping. And other than umbrellas and towels, the most reliable comfort purchase was the mop.

Business at Brennick's Mop Emporium had never been better. Viola had learned every model by name and purpose—the SwishMaster 2000, the Super-Absorbent Wonder Mop, the S2000 Ergonomic Wet Broom, and the mysterious Deluxe Spin-Dry Hydra-Head, which occasionally came to life if left too long in the bucket.

She recited their virtues cheerfully to every customer who came dripping through the door. And, as Mr. Brennick liked to say, "Listening is half the sale." So she listened—about the locusts, about the merfolk, about the boggarts, about the sheep shortage, about the pricklepepper crisis, and about how nothing worked the way it used to.

By closing time, the complaints were mopped up, the shelves restocked, and everyone felt slightly better.

Things, after all, could always be worse.

Or so they thought.

Viola came in with her scarf soaked and shoes squelching, but her usual cheer faltered the moment she saw her mother. She was just sitting at the table, hands folded, eyes fixed on the middle distance like someone trying to remember something important that had just been stolen.

Viola hung up her scarf to dry and sat down quietly. "So... how was your day?" she asked, as cheerfully as possible.

"Oh, it was good," her mother said, smiling tiredly—the kind of tired that had nothing to do with walking or working or weather, and everything to do with the end of something dear.

Viola followed her gaze to the stove.

There was no pot. No bubbling. No ladle. No steam.

A truly ominous silence.

She went from nervous to alarmed. "So... what would you like for dinner?" she asked.

Her mother sighed, eyes wistful. "Spicy clam chowder," she said. "Oh... I love that."

Viola stood up at once. Whatever had knocked the joy out of her mother, she thought, could surely be fixed with soup.

And, in fairness, this belief is not unique to Dampenia. Across the world, soup is often the first line of defence against sorrow. But in Dampenia, it is more than true. It is gospel.

Now, to make a spicy clam chowder, you need:

• bacon

• clams

• potatoes

• garlic

• onion

• butter

- cream

- flour

- salt

- pricklepepper (lots)

Viola set about gathering what she could. Ham—not bacon, but close. Clams—small, a little old, but willing. Potatoes—slightly rubbery, but fine. Butter—good. Milk—instead of cream, but that would do.

She chopped, stirred, hummed to herself, and opened the spice cupboard.

Then paused. Then stared. Then opened it wider, as if that might somehow change the outcome.

It was bare.

No jars. No backup tin. Not even a sachet of emergency flakes.

No pricklepepper.

A chill deeper than the rain settled over her. Now she understood. Now she knew why her mother had looked like the sky was falling. Because, in a way, it had.

She turned around slowly. "Mum... where's the pricklepepper?"

Her mother didn't answer right away.

Then, very gently, she reached into her coat pocket and placed something on the table.

A single pepper. Wrinkled. Red. Glorious.

Viola blinked. "Is... is that the last one?"

Her mother nodded. "Everywhere was sold out. People were hoarding it. Someone broke into Grebblestone's Grocer and stole every last pinch. I was there when it happened. I couldn't do anything."

She looked down at her hand, still curled slightly from where she'd clutched it the whole walk home. "I grabbed one. Just one. And I held on."

Viola whispered, "The cupboard was full last week..."

"They've eaten the plants," her mother said quietly. "Not just the peppers—the stalks. The roots. The whole harvest. The Brean locusts got them."

Viola sat down slowly. "All of them?"

Her mother nodded. "Every last one. There's nothing left. Not in the shops. Not in the fields. Not in the royal gardens. The price has gone mad. People are trying to buy them in secret, like it's spice-smuggling season again. But there's nothing to buy. It's gone."

Gone.

Dampenia without pricklepepper was like soup without salt.

Rain without clouds.

Tragedy without music.

They hadn't just eaten the spice. They had eaten the national identity.

Viola stared at the lonely little pepper sitting on the table. It gleamed in the lamplight like a ruby—or a warning.

They had one left. One.

She picked it up carefully, holding it in her hands like it might bruise.

"What do we do?" she asked.

Her mother looked at the potless stove and said, "We wait." Then after a pause, added, "And don't let anyone find it."

Chapter 6

o one quite knew what to do.

The citizens gathered in the town square, dejected. Some were so low they didn't even bother to raise their umbrellas.

The royal town crier emerged from the castle, climbed the slick steps, and unrolled a scroll.

"His Royal Eminence, King Darius III, Monarch of Luminescence, Lord of Sunshine, Omni-Potent and Suchly, and so forth—"

A few Dampenians brightened.

"Ah!" said someone hopefully. "At last!"

"…having noted the lack of zip in his omelette, and having found the whole thing bland, unpleasant, and hardly worth eating…"

Nods all around. "He understands."

"…and having been informed that the royal cupboards are thoroughly barren of spice of any variety…"

An audible gasp.

"…the royal chef having confessed to diluting His Lordship's meals through the wrongful substitution of Molgorodian jalapeños—"

A few boos.

"—and occasionally Crackendorian bonnets."

"Oh!" said the same few, unsure if that was worse or better.

"…and repeated efforts to acquire proper pepperage having failed despite diligence and perseverance…"

A voice called, "Hear, hear!" Another added, "That's the spirit!" Then both fell silent when they realized nothing had yet been promised.

"…and Merwin having exhausted all avenues of advice…"

No one mentioned Merwin's usual record.

"…His Royal Highness doth here declare that there shall be convened a royal committee to assess this national state of emergency…"

A cautious cheer rippled through the square.

"…and issue a report recommending potential plans of action…"

The cheer thinned.

"…to solve the crisis, no matter how severe or extreme…"

It rose again, briefly.

"…so long as they are not too expensive so as to exhaust the treasury."

Pffft. The sound came from someone's umbrella, but it felt collective.

"…and that anyone with the will to nominate themselves or their neighbour to said committee shall immediately put forth their name…"

A murmur of mild confusion. No one appeared willing to volunteer themselves. A few pointed at each other questioningly.

"…to be considered to form a subcommittee for the selection of persons more appropriate, on an urgent basis…"

Now no one spoke at all.

"…while remaining calm."

The crier let the scroll droop.

There was a moment of silence. Then a sort of damp, reluctant applause—the kind that happens when people clap mostly to prove they're still alive.

Around them, Dampenians murmured in cautious agreement. A few optimists nodded approvingly, already imagining the minutes, the motions, the small sense of progress that came from sitting in circles. Others just looked at the puddles collecting around their boots and wondered if anything would ever dry again.

The crier rolled up his scroll, bowed mechanically, and trudged back toward the castle. His feather drooped.

Viola clapped too, because she believed in being polite to criers.

Her mother didn't. She folded her umbrella neatly and said, "Committees. Always committees."

"Do you think they'll fix it?" Viola asked.

"They'll discuss fixing it, dear," her mother said. "Which is nearly the same thing, only slower."

Viola considered this carefully. "So… next week, then?"

Her mother smiled faintly. "Next year, if the minutes are approved."

Viola considered. She wasn't sure whether that was good or bad, but it certainly wasn't spicy.

Chapter 7

It was around this time that Viola decided she needed to do something.

Not because she thought herself a hero, but because she figured—in a shockingly un-Dampenian way—that if one did something about a problem, the problem might get better.

She didn't sneak off. At breakfast (which had been reduced to a bowl of boiled carrots and salt) she told her mother what she planned. Her mother, halfway through packing her work-umbrella, nodded absently and said, "Mm-hmm," in the same tone she used for shopping lists and small disasters. Viola took this as approval. Technically, it was.

Then she told Mr. Brennick she needed the day off. He wasn't pleased, of course. But when she assured him that she'd already alphabetized the mops—including the new shipment of Magical Molvo's Easy-Dry Zwifters—he relented and said she could take the afternoon, which was really quite generous of him.

Which was how, by midday, she was squelching down a muddy lane bordered by dripping shrubs, on her way to find the King of the Brean Locusts.

The rain was not falling so much as leaning—sideways, insistently, with professional dedication. It was the sort that found the gap at the back of your collar and settled, cold and smug, against your spine; that slapped your cheeks just to watch you blink. It played in the mud until the ground became a sticky paste and your shoes accumulated great heavy clods around your ankles, making each step a negotiation. The sky resembled dishwater after a long argument. It was the sort of day where Dampenians, passing each other, might nod and say, "Rain coming in, I think," or possibly, "Beautiful day, isn't it?"

Halfway down the lane, she noticed a boy.

He was sitting beside a body of water that could not quite decide whether it was a puddle or a pond. He held a fishing pole and stared quietly at the line where it vanished into the grey surface.

He looked about her age: thin and pale, with hair that might once have attempted curls but had since given up, lain down to rest, and never gotten back up again. He had a hunch to his back that made his posture look like someone caught mid-dive into the pond before him—paused there, permanently.

Viola considered the pondlet. It was roughly the size of a horse lying down, and about as likely to contain fish.

Not wanting to be rude, she stopped and asked, "Catching anything?"

He didn't look up. "Nope. It's hopeless." His voice was low and warm, but he spoke slowly, with sadness, pausing to sigh between statements.

She stepped closer. "Are you sure this is a good spot?"

He turned to her. He had a wide nose, big ears, and thick lips. It was a nice face, a kindly face, though there was something tragic about it—the sort of face that expected rain and was never disappointed.

"About as good as any place," he answered with a sigh.

She smiled. "Piddle River is just up ahead, I think. Might be better? At least a fish could actually reach it." She waved her finger in a circle to indicate the pondlet's complete isolation. "This one doesn't seem to have a way for fish to get in."

"Piddle's fished out," he said, turning back to the water and bobbing his line. "All the good spots are taken by the merfolk."

Viola crouched beside him. The puddle-pond was perfectly still, a grey mirror reflecting grey sky. "Are there even fish in there?"

"Doubt it," he said. "But if there were, they wouldn't bite. Why would they? Everything's doomed."

"I suppose," she said. "But that doesn't mean we have to give up."

Then, suddenly, she realized something. "Say—you haven't given up! You're still fishing even though it's hopeless."

He made a face. "I gave up three weeks ago."

"Then why are you still here?"

He thought for a long moment. Finally, he said, "Well, if everything's hopeless, what's the point of stopping?"

She nodded, approving of his logic. "I like you. What's your name?"

"Pall."

"I'm Viola. Why don't you come with me? I'm going to find the King of the Brean Locusts to fix the pricklepepper problem."

He gave her a look of pure disbelief. "Locusts can't talk."

"Has anyone tried?"

"No," he admitted. "But they can't."

"Well then, we'll see," Viola said brightly.

He sighed. "There's no point."

"There never is," she said, "until there is."

He frowned at that. "You sound optimistic."

"I'm not. I'm practical." She stood, offering her hand. "Come on. I'll help you find a better fishing spot on the way."

He hesitated. "Why?"

"Because doing something hopeless together is better than doing it alone?"

He stared at the water, then at the sky, then at her hand. Finally, with the slow reluctance of someone who expects disappointment but refuses to rush toward it, he took it.

"Fine," he said, standing. "But when this fails, I'm going to say I told you so."

"That's the spirit," Viola said.

She wasn't entirely sure it was, but it seemed close enough.

Chapter 8

Viola and Pall trudged along the muddy hedge road in search of the King of the Brean—a plan she had, to be fair, not thought through. She did not know where the king lived, or even if there was one. Also, her stomach was already reminding her that boiled carrots and half a loaf of bread were not enough to quest upon.

By the time the clouds had slouched halfway across the afternoon, hunger had become insistent.

"Say," she asked, "do you happen to have anything to eat?"

As it turned out, Pall had a few things and, despite his gloomy demeanour, was kindly—or resigned— enough to share what he had. He produced a small wedge of cheese, an apple, and some slightly soggy crackers.

"Help yourself. It was going bad anyway."

They found a flat stone under a tree that served as a makeshift table, spread out a handkerchief, and settled down for a simple picnic.

"Where are you from?" Viola asked.

"Wimpishire."

"Is it nice?"

"It's fine," he said. "If you like dreary and miserable." He sliced the apple into quarters. "You?"

"Dropminster."

"Oh. A fancy person."

"It's not all fancy castles," she said. "Mum and I are regular."

She took another bite, considering the mix of sharp cheese and wilted cracker a success. "Have you ever been to the capital?"

"No." He raised his hand toward his shoulder as if to say, *I don't think they'd like a hunchback.*

Viola was thinking how best to respond when she noticed a tiny newcomer at the foot of their picnic stone: a small Brean locust.

The Brean look approximately like grasshoppers—if grasshoppers were dressed and walked upright. They are particular creatures. They can spend an hour a day polishing their heads, choosing the right hat, and adjusting their antennae just so—only to ruin it by noon through their uncontrollable appetites.

This one was about the size of a thumb, wore muddy boots, a red sweater, and the smallest fisherman's hat Viola had ever seen. He peered up at them wistfully, antennae twitching.

"Good afternoon," she said.

He bowed and rubbed his legs together, producing a high-pitched buzz that was probably something gracious in Locus.

Pall scowled and covered the food, then kicked at the little fellow. "Shoo!"

The little creature hopped back, crestfallen.

"Don't scare him," Viola said. "He's just hungry."

"He's a locust. They're always hungry."

He was, in fact, starving. A misjudged hop and a rogue gust had blown him several farms away from home. He had spent the better part of a day and a half hopping aimlessly with nothing but the odd leaf for sustenance—which was not ideal, as he had an allergy to green leafy vegetables. Not fatal, but very uncomfortable.

"Don't be afraid," she called out. "I'm sure we have a little for you." She broke off a piece of cracker and held it out.

He perked up but stood cautiously, watching Pall.

"He's afraid of you."

Pall started wrapping up their picnic. "I'm not letting him eat my food."

"All right," Viola said. She held out the tiny snack—which, though small for a human, was still half the size of the locust.

The locust licked his lips and hopped tentatively forward. Then stopped again and looked at Pall's foot.

"Tell him you won't hurt him."

Pall hunched. "Fine. I won't."

That was enough. The locust hopped forward and devoured the cracker in one ecstatic blur, scattering crumbs like fireworks.

"My word," said Viola.

"I've a bad feeling about this," said Pall.

The Brean brushed off his face and sweater, straightened his hat, and clapped his hands twice—a gesture that could have meant thanks or declaration of war. Then he hopped up onto her shoulder. She was startled for a moment until she heard the tiniest high-pitched buzz in her ear.

Bzz bzz.

It sounded, if you were the sort of person inclined to hear the best in things, rather like "thank you."

Viola smiled. "You're very welcome. What's your name?"

The locust buzzed proudly: *Bzz-click-bzz-bzz-click-click-bzz-bzz-bzz-click-click-bzz-click-bzz-bzz*…and continued in the same vein for about a minute.

Locusts, being insects, do not have human names. Like most insect races, there are far too many of them to have names as we do. Instead, they are sorted and categorized in math and numbered. This little guy was named 93998544771114356.

"Oh," said Viola. "That's quite long, isn't it? Do you mind if I call you Tim instead?"

The locust paused, antennae twitching thoughtfully. Then he shrugged—an impressive gesture for someone with shoulders the size of peppercorns—and buzzed twice.

Viola smiled. "See? We've made a friend."

Pall groaned. "We've adopted an appetite."

It was, Viola thought, a fair trade.

Chapter 9

y late afternoon the road grew busier, and the fields on either side looked strangely bitten—not chewed exactly, but nibbled, as though a very polite army of something had taken one bite from every stalk before moving on.

Viola frowned. "Do you think that's the start of the locust problem?"

Pall nodded, studying a corn stalk that appeared to have been sampled rather than eaten. "Probably sampling for later. Or hoping the taste improves."

"Or quality control," Viola suggested.

"I doubt anyone asked for it. Also, no one can understand their opinion."

Tim, perched on Viola's shoulder, rubbed his legs together in what she had learned meant either *Yes*, No, or *The quality is clearly poor, since the crops are still standing.* Tim's opinions, she'd noticed, were generally correct but rarely helpful.

"How long before they come back and eat the rest?" she asked.

Pall glanced at the horizon, where a faint shimmer suggested something moving in numbers. "About a week. Maybe less if someone insults their queen."

"Do locusts have queens? Or kings?"

"Whichever is worse, that's what they probably have."

"Tim, do you know?"

Tim hopped down onto her hand, held up his tiny two-fingered hands to his forehead, turned his head proudly, and batted his eyes.

"Queen then!"

Tim clapped. Viola thought they were really making progress.

"Well, then, let's go find her. Do you happen to know where she is?"

Tim chittered for about half a minute, then shrugged.

"Of course he doesn't," Pall said. "That would be too easy."

Tim seemed unimpressed with himself.

"That's okay, Tim," Viola said, continuing on. "We'll just ask around. I'm sure someone knows where she is."

By dinnertime the trio reached a town called Dripmere—the sort of place that produced turnips, puddles, and complaints about both. Smoke leaned sideways in the rain as if it too were trying to leave. A few lamps blinked on, wondering if anyone would notice.

In the square stood a stone well, and beside it a creature of sheer elegance and evident despair. A Fae woman—silver hair catching the lamplight, a tiny blue coat that had clearly never heard of practicality or modesty, and jewellery that gleamed even through the rain—now stood soaked and spattered with mud.

The people of the town gave her an extremely wide berth.

Viola, being Viola, went straight to her. "Hello! Miss? Are you all right?"

The Fae looked up, managing to appear both magnificent and miserable. "It's Shesay," she answered, indicating herself with a scaled hand and wiping away beautiful tears. "And no! Not remotely." Her voice sounded like silk that had seen hard use. "I've suffered a catastrophe."

"Oh dear," said Viola, because one should always take other people's catastrophes seriously. "Whatever has happened?"

"I have dropped my nose ring into this horrid well."

Pall peered down the shaft. Water glimmered somewhere far below, utterly uninterested in returning anything. "Well, that's gone."

"Yes," Shesay agreed mournfully. "And the ring was beautiful. Given to me by a friend who loved me more than life itself."

That indeed was a tragedy.

"Could we climb down?" Viola suggested.

"Too narrow," Pall said, testing the stones. "You'd get stuck about eight feet down."

"Too wet. And dirty," added Shesay with a delicate shudder. "And wells hate me. Especially this one. I may have said some things to it earlier."

"To the well?"

"It's not my fault. It was being difficult!"

Viola leaned over the edge. The darkness below seemed to lean back, considering her. "What did you say to it?"

"I said…" She stopped and leaned close to whisper, so the well could not hear, "it was a useless pretender, and no one would ever swim in it."

"Ah."

"And that's why it stole my nose ring."

"I see," said Viola, though to be honest, she didn't exactly. Wells, as you know, do not have hands and do not steal nose rings or anything else, unless one happens to drop something into them. Which was, more likely, what had actually happened.

Shesay gestured dramatically. "Now it's keeping my ring out of spite."

Viola turned to Tim, who had been following the conversation with the patient interest of someone who already knew how it would end. "Tim?"

Tim rubbed his legs together thoughtfully: *Obviously.*

Moments later he was seated in the bucket—an old wooden thing that had lowered turnips, raised water, and never expected to transport heroes—antennae quivering with barely suppressed heroism as the villagers gathered at a cautious distance. A thin fishing line was tied round his waist for safety.

"You're sure about this?" Pall asked. "Probably not safetied for this use."

Tim adjusted his hat with the dignity of a ship's captain.

"Right then," said Viola. "Ready?"

Tim clapped his hands once, firmly.

Down he went, squeaking faintly against the rope. The bucket rattled against stone and disappeared into blackness. After a bit, the rope went slack.

They waited.

The villagers waited.

Somewhere, a dog forgot what it was barking at.

"How long can locusts hold their breath?" asked a man with spectacular eyebrows.

"Longer than you might think?" said Pall, though he didn't actually know.

Then Shesay said, "He's calling."

Fae have far better hearing than humans.

So they hauled him back up, hand over hand. Tim emerged dripping, wings plastered to his sides, and immediately launched into a very energetic performance involving flailing arms, hopping in circles, and falling down repeatedly.

"There's bats in the well?" Viola guessed.

"You're covered with a rash?" Pall guessed.

"The water was slimy and disgusting?" suggested Shesay.

Tim shook himself vigorously and tried again. They called out what he pantomimed:

"You're playing drums." No.

"Going down the well." Yes!

"There was a splash." Yes!

"You're drowning." Yes!

"Can't swim!" Viola realized. "Of course! Tim, why didn't you say?"

Tim gave her a look that suggested this was rich, coming from someone with proper arms.

"We need a different approach," Pall said, already pulling fishing line from his pack. "Something that doesn't require aquatic skills."

"Or that involves fewer theatrical re-enactments," Shesay murmured.

After some discussion, one brief argument about knot types, and a short incident involving a borrowed ladle and a very confused baker, they devised a plan. Pall tied thread to the fishing line, bent a hook just so, and lowered it into the dark. Tim went too this time—riding the bucket again but armed with thread—issuing a series of shrill, bossy squeaks that echoed up the shaft.

"He said left," Shesay translated.

"Now he's saying, 'No, your left!'"

They adjusted.

The crowd leaned in. Rain dripped steadily in a rhythm of patience. Somewhere, a cow lowed in what might have been suspense, or possibly just cows being cows.

Then a jerk on the line.

A collective intake of breath.

The line came up, and then he was there—Tim the triumphant, bearing a glimmer of gold.

Shesay gasped. "My ring!" She seized it, kissed it, and then—out of sheer gratitude and also because she was Fae and didn't particularly care about mortal conventions—kissed everyone within reach. Viola blushed crimson. Pall went rigid as a fence post. Tim preened magnificently.

The townsmen, who had been maintaining their distance, suddenly found reasons to assist with coiling rope and returning buckets. Their wives arrived moments later to collect them, muttering things about "certain types" and "that coat" and "honestly, Gerald."

Left standing in the square, Shesay sighed theatrically. "Humans," she said, swaying her hips. "So easily enchanted, and so poorly organized about it."

Viola smiled, wringing water from her sleeve. "It's getting late. I should probably head home."

"Nonsense," said Shesay, brightening like a lamp someone had just trimmed. "My family's caravan is just outside town. You shall dine with us. It's the least I can do. Well, it's not technically the least—I could just say thank you and leave—but dinner is more interesting."

Pall gave Viola a doubtful look that said *we should absolutely not do this*.

Viola gave him her usual hopeful one.

"There will be fish," Shesay added, reading the silence perfectly.

And so, with the rain turning silvery in the lamplight and Tim riding Viola's shoulder like a tiny, damp general, they followed the Fae as she slid through the town and led them toward the edge of Dripmere— toward lanterns that flickered in the mist like curious eyes and voices that promised more adventure than was strictly advisable.

"I'm starting to think," Pall muttered, "that you have a terrible sense of danger."

"I prefer to think of it as hope," Viola replied.

"Those are the same thing."

"Not if it works out in the end."

Behind them, the well burped once, spitefully, and returned to being a hole in the ground.

Chapter 10

he Fae caravan shimmered at the edge of Dripmere like a row of jewel boxes that had decided to lounge about and not pay any taxes. Lanterns swayed from poles shaped like coral branches. Music rose from somewhere deep inside: a harp, a flute, and something that hissed politely when struck.

Viola had never seen anything like it.

Shesay slid between the wagons with the grandeur of someone introducing her own brilliance. Each wagon gleamed in marine colours—turquoise, coral, silver— and smelled faintly of salt and cinnamon. Merlings darted about, sleek and curious, tails flicking, laughter rippling like water.

"Your homes are beautiful," Viola said.

"Of course," Shesay replied. "We have excellent taste. We're Fae."

That, apparently, explained everything.

Inside a great tent draped with shells, they found cushions, steaming platters of raw fish, and more cats than could possibly be justified. The cats reclined on tables, cushions, and one another, watching the newcomers with half-opened eyes and disdain.

"They help with the fish," Shesay said. "And the magic."

"What sort of magic?" Viola asked.

The cats pretended they hadn't heard.

"Cats never reveal their magic," came a voice, and the matriarch emerged—a broad-tailed elder with a voice like polished coral. "Shesay, who are our guests?"

Shesay hadn't asked their names, so she made them up.

"This is Mary, with her pet locust, Handy. And the boy, Chorch."

"That's not—"

But the matriarch smiled broadly and talked over her. "Of course, of course. I'm Aishiesiaochisssah. But I understand humans have very simple tongues, so you may call me Empress."

"Are you an empress?" Viola asked, very impressed.

"But of course."

She was not.

Viola curtsied, uncertain how to behave.

Empress smiled, delighted. "Now aren't you a dear. Let's eat!"

Dinner began—or possibly a performance involving food. The Fae didn't cook; they composed. Slices of fish shimmered on glass plates, dusted with seaweed and something faintly sweet. There were sweets of kelp and condensed milk—alarming to behold, delightful to taste.

Pall leaned close and whispered, "This isn't cooked. Don't eat it or you'll get sick."

Tim didn't wait. He hopped down and polished off two morsels in an instant. Fish splashed everywhere and the cats hissed. So did some of the Fae. Tim, terrified, scurried up Viola's arm and hid under her collar, quivering.

Viola wasn't even sure how to eat it. The merfolk delicately speared theirs with their claws.

The matriarch noticed. "Shesay, they don't have claws."

The Fae leaned in, fascinated. The matriarch took Viola's hand, turning it over, delighted by its strangeness. In the end, one of the merlings presented them with tiny spiral horns with which to skewer the fish.

Viola took a few careful bites. "This is wonderful! Pall, you must try it!"

Pall eyed it warily, but at her insistence took a bite.

"I suppose it's nice—for foreign food. Would be better boiled with pricklepepper."

The tent gasped.

"Boiled? Disgusting," said one of the merlings.

"I'm sorry," Viola said quickly. "We don't mean to offend."

"It's fine, my dear," said the matriarch. "Dry-folk have such odd customs. But I do agree that the loss of the pricklepepper is a tragedy." Her eyes slid to Viola's collar with quiet menace. "Filthy little locusts. Proper races do not eat like gluttons."

Viola changed the subject, deciding not to argue with their host. "We're actually on our way to find their queen—to explain that they've caused a huge crisis."

Silence. Then brittle laughter, like breaking glass.

"The tiny devourers," someone said. "Oh, little dry one. You don't know, do you?"

"Know what?" Viola asked.

Empress set down her cup. "The songs are very old," she said. "They tell of countless small ones who came to Atlantis. They ate the gardens, the fields, the roots beneath the land itself. And Atlantis sank."

Rain tapped on the canvas.

Tim popped out, clearly offended. He rubbed his legs furiously.

The Fae leaned in. Shesay waved a hand. "He says that's not what happened. But this was centuries ago, little hopper. And what about your little eating display a moment ago? Are you sure your people would never do such a thing?"

Tim's antennae drooped, and he sat down, defeated.

Viola's throat tightened. "Where is the Queen now? If we could talk to her—"

"Talk?" The matriarch's laugh was soft, not kind. "Child, the Queen hides where no one can reach her. If she dies, every locust dies."

Tim made a small, broken noise and looked up in shock.

"The Mouth of Doom," whispered a merling. "It's a whirlpool in the Sea of Flumes. Ships vanish there. They say the Queen sits at its heart."

"No human can go there and live," Shesay said. "But they keep trying. The sea is littered with wrecks."

Tim's small body quivered; faint squeaks of grief escaped him.

"Of course you didn't know," said the matriarch. "Your lives are very short and mostly filled with eating. We Fae, on the other hand, travel the worlds and fill our souls with knowledge."

Tim crawled down Viola's arm and tapped urgently on her wrist—a private message, hidden from the Fae's knowing eyes. His movements were jagged, uncertain. Viola didn't need translation: *Would I die too?*

She had no answer.

Pall, who had been quietly nibbling, set down his skewer. "Well. That's that."

"What do you mean?" Viola asked.

"I mean we need to head home. The Brean Queen is in a whirlpool. We're kids—and a locust."

"But—"

"Viola." His voice cracked. "The Sea of Flumes is miles north. We don't have a boat, or know how to sail. And even if we did, the ships wreck. It's a ship-eating whirlpool."

The matriarch regarded them with pity and amusement. "Stay here, little dry one. Let the adults handle such things."

It was tempting. She could stay—sleep in a sea-painted wagon, learn secret magic from cats, forget the whirlpool, the famine, the Crown.

Then, quietly, she said, "The adults aren't handling it. That's why I left."

"Viola," said Pall, "be reasonable. It's impossible."

"I just think that maybe…"

"You could sail into a whirlpool?" He laughed once, sharply. "I'm not brave like you. I'm just—" He stopped, glancing at the Fae, who were politely ignoring him. "Just the ugly boy who follows you because you're kind."

Viola wanted to tell him he was wrong but couldn't find the words. Because he wasn't wrong about how they'd treated him—the Fae had spoken about him, not to him. Shesay had seated him in the shadows, served him last, smiled past his face all evening.

"You're not—" she began, then stopped. What could she say? That he wasn't ugly? That would make it about his face, not the problem.

"You don't have to come," she said finally, knowing it was the wrong thing even as she said it.

She wished she could unsay it, but words, once dampened, tend to stick.

Pall opened his mouth, closed it. His expression did something complicated that made Viola's chest hurt.

The matriarch sighed. "Brave and foolish often wear the same face," she murmured. "Drink, child. You'll need strength."

She snapped her fingers and small cups of wine were passed around. A hot, spicy aroma rose from the cups.

"Thank you, but we're not adults."

"Very well," said Empress. One of the merlings added water. Viola had meant they weren't allowed to drink at all, but now it seemed rude not to, since it had been prepared especially for them.

Viola sipped. It was hot and burny and made her feel taller.

Tim, too small for a cup, sat on the rim, used his hat as a bowl, and drank far too much. At one point he tried to stand to make an announcement but fell in and had to be fished out.

The Fae found this uproariously funny, and the tension cracked.

Stories became songs; songs became boasts.

A young merman with a shell-lute appeared and composed an anthem for Shesay.

It was about Crackendor, and the chorus went something like this:

"Who's the bore? Crackendor! dum-dah dum-dah dum-dah dum!"

It was awful, but Shesay enjoyed the attention. She clapped brightly and forgot our heroes existed.

Viola leaned back, eyes heavy, watching lanternlight ripple over silk.

Pall sat hunched at the edge of the cushions, staring at nothing.

She thought of her mother by the window, of Mr. Brennick and his mop racks, of Atlantis sinking and the Mouth of Doom roaring unseen.

"We really should be going," she mumbled.

The matriarch whistled. Three cats rose, stretched, and vanished into the rain.

"They'll tell your parents where you are," she said. "Whether they deliver the right message is another matter."

Viola decided not to worry. She was too sleepy to worry. Too sleepy to think of whirlpools or Pall's hurt face or the weight of a kingdom.

Thunder muttered. The lute rambled into its seventeenth verse. The cats remained mysterious. And the rain fell, as it always did in Dampenia— softly, endlessly, and without apology.

Before she could decide anything at all, Viola was asleep.

Chapter 11

iola woke beneath a mountain of blankets so vividly patterned they might have been stolen from a carnival. A small cat had installed itself on her stomach and was purring industriously, using her as a source of heat. She lay still, uncertain whether moving would be impolite.

Nearby, Tim stood on the table in nothing but his undergarments, attempting to wash his shirt in a saucer with all the dignity of an insect performing a deeply private ritual. His antennae drooped. His wings hung limp. He looked both embarrassed and slightly ill—which, given how much cinnamon-scented Fae wine he had drunk the night before, seemed fair.

He suddenly realized she was watching, made a little buzz of dismay, and frantically hopped inside an empty cup to hide his nakedness.

"I didn't see anything," Viola lied.

Pall slept in the far corner, curled like a damp question mark, his blanket half-kicked away. She thought about pulling it back over him but decided against it—he'd only kick it off again. In the pale light he looked oddly arranged. Not ugly. Just… bent. Large eyes, lashes far too long for a boy that gloomy, hair the colour of wet bread crust curling against his forehead. He reminded her of a prince who had been slightly smushed by mistake.

She stood and wrapped a small patchwork blanket around her shoulders like a shawl. The cat mewed in protest.

Outside, the morning was a sort of light—thin, undecided, and doing its best. The rain had paused, like someone making tea before returning to their book.

The glamour of the night had vanished. The caravans that had shimmered like jewels now sagged, their colours dulled to the grey-brown of old dishwater. Broken wheels and cracked boards lay scattered about, and someone had strung washing lines between two wagons, heavy with dripping garments. Fae magic, apparently, didn't extend to carpentry.

Viola pulled her shawl tighter and looked north. The hills rolled away in soft folds, damp and grey-green. Here and there, small farms clung to the slopes like stubborn barnacles, their fields fenced with crooked posts. Beyond them, darker woods gathered, pooling around the horizon. Somewhere far past all that— past the trees and the distance and the mist—lay the sea, and possibly the Queen of the Brean, sitting on her whirlpool throne in the heart of a storm that devoured ships. And even if she was there, and even if Viola somehow reached her, there was no promise she'd stop her people from eating the Dampenians out of house and home—and peppers.

She thought of her mother. By now she'd be at the castle, sleeves rolled, elbows-deep in someone else's linen. She had started years ago as an underwear scrubber, working her way up through a hierarchy of fabrics: underwear, towels, pants, tablecloths, sheets, and eventually—through diligence and sheer endurance—delicates. It was a career of distinction.

Her mother never complained. When Viola's father died, she had held her umbrella straight, dry-eyed, patting Viola's hand. "Tut-tut, my dear," she'd said. "You get what you get. Crying won't bring him back." Then she'd gone home and made soup. Ten pricklepeppers went into the pot—enough heat to make hair rise and eyes run. Neighbours came with spoons and condolences. They all said he'd been a decent chap. Everyone's eyes watered, which was considered both good manners and good seasoning.

That was the Dampenian way. The pepper made crying respectable. It appeared at births, baptisms, first-umbrella ceremonies, weddings, first disasters, tenth disasters, and, of course, deaths.

Now there were no pricklepeppers left. No proper seasoning. No proper way to cry.

Viola stood there in the thin drizzle and cried anyway—impolitely, without seasoning. A pale ribbon of light crept down between the clouds as if it had noticed.

She thought about the Mouth of Doom. How large was a whirlpool, really? Bigger than a ship, certainly. Maybe ten ships. And she was smaller than one ship. Much smaller. What could she possibly do?

Pall was right. It was impossible.

Yet the tears didn't make her want to stop. They cleared something inside her, the way rain clears smoke.

Behind her, the caravan door creaked open. Pall appeared, hair sticking up, eyes half open. He blinked at the sky as if personally offended by its brightness.

"You're up early," he said.

"I couldn't sleep."

He stood beside her, following her gaze north. For a long moment, neither spoke. The hills darkened and brightened in turns as clouds moved overhead.

"I think I'm going," she said at last. "To see the sea. Just to look."

"Just to look," he repeated slowly. "And if the Queen of the Brean happens to rise out of it?"

"Then I'll think of something polite to say."

He frowned. "What about your job?"

"Mr. Brennick will understand. Probably. Eventually. I'll send an apology through the Empress. She handles delicate matters."

"You shouldn't go alone."

"I'm not asking you to come."

"I know." He looked down at his hands. "But

no one will miss me. People don't like hunchbacks. They think we bring bad luck. They don't say it to your face, but they cross the street. Make signs against evil when they think you're not looking."

She turned to face him properly. "That's not true. Pall, you're not unlucky."

"Maybe not. But people aren't like you, Viola."

The way he said her name made something tighten in her chest. He reached for her hand, tentative, as if asking permission. She didn't pull away. The touch was warm and real and ordinary in the best possible way.

"Well then," she said. "We'll both be unlucky together. That should balance things out."

The corner of his mouth twitched—almost a smile.

Rain began again—softly at first, then with more conviction.

"We'll need umbrellas," he said.

"Two," she agreed.

The day sloshed lightly around them, but she held on to him and felt steadier.

"Nothing's impossible," she said, turning north again.

Pall opened his mouth to correct her, then just sighed instead.

He sighed, and she smiled. The rain, after all, had excellent timing.

Chapter 12

hey set out after a light breakfast, which in merfolk households means leftovers. This morning they had leftover seaweed, sweet milk, and opinions.

At the gate, the matriarch pressed gifts upon them: two umbrellas apparently re-invented by merfolk—patched with bright cloth and trimmed with what looked like gold but proved to be merely wood painted rather convincingly. She also waved forward a pair of merlings who presented packets of seaweed tied with ribbon.

"For the road," she said.

Viola and Pall opened the umbrellas and marvelled at the riot of colour. Viola twirled and laughed. Pall frowned.

"Are you sure there isn't one that's grey? I'd rather not resemble a bouquet."

The matriarch ignored him.

Viola curtsied as best she could. She had no practice in curtsying, but she did her best, as such behaviour seemed appropriate before an Empress. "Your gracious Empress, thank you ever so much for your kindness and your help. Did my mother truly get the message?"

The matriarch made a dismissive wave. "Don't call me Empress—that was only last night, dear. And yes, your mother received word. In return for word of your heroism, she sent advice about rain boots, keeping dry, and not making a scene—very sensible things. You may ignore all of it."

Shesay hugged Viola goodbye and murmured, far too audibly, "He's nice, but you can do better."

Viola didn't know what that meant and wasn't sure it was nice. She thanked the mermaid anyway. As her mother always said, manners cost less than quarrels.

Two caravan cats escorted them down the lane—or possibly were simply heading that way. After fifty yards they lost interest and went to chase mice.

North lay a country of soft folds and reluctant stone, the sort of land that stayed green from habit. The road, when it appeared, was two wheel tracks with grass between. Hedges dripped. Hills hunched. Clouds looked about for anywhere unwatered and promptly corrected it.

Viola skipped and hummed a tune that arrived fully formed in her head, light as a kettle beginning to think about boiling.

"What song is that?" Pall asked.

"I don't know," she said. "A country rain song, I think."

"Can you teach it to me?"

"I would, but I don't know how it goes."

And he had to be content with that.

Fields rolled by. Sheep regarded them briefly. Barley stood in neat ranks except where it didn't. Here and there whole patches of crop had vanished—bare earth where once pricklepepper had grown. The gaps looked polite, which didn't make them less alarming.

"Breans," Pall said.

Tim's antennae wilted. He rubbed his legs together in a muted chord of apology.

By mid-afternoon they reached a small town crouched between two hills at a river fork. One hill grazed sheep; the other held a forest—though part of that forest had decided to move down and stand beside the river. Unfortunately, that was where the town had been.

Outside the town there had once stood a stone statue and a sign that read, *"Master Arbuthsump, Founding Father of Sumpford."* Only the base remained, which read merely *Sump*. The rest had relocated.

The cause was plain. Gideon Poplars were striding through the streets.

Gideon Poplars are a spirited kind of tree that, when suitably aroused, are prone to wandering. They range from tiny sprouts to hundred-foot ancients. Unable to see, they feel

their way by root and branch. Having escaped the forest, they appeared to think houses were large saplings in need of rearrangement. They shouldered them aside with leafy politeness. The houses voiced their disapproval by cracking and falling down.

Townsfolk darted among the trunks carrying kettles, clocks, and one elderly goose who refused rescue.

A thin man in spectacles and an ink-stained coat hurried past, muttering figures under his breath.

"Excuse me—what's happening?" Viola called.

He blinked, grateful for an audience. "Half the bakery front, two-thirds the bakery back, smithy roof relocated, apothecary presently beneath tree No. 7, mayor's office unaccounted for, and the Founder's statue seeking a better view."

He turned a page with solemn care. "Sorry. I'm the Mayor-Accountant. Somewhat preoccupied today, on account of our leafy neighbours deciding to inhabit the town. My lists keep needing revision."

Across the square, the blacksmith was desperately trying to rescue his anvil as a Gideon Poplar, working with great delicacy, lifted his chimney off to improve ventilation.

"Why are they here?" Pall asked.

"No one knows," said the Mayor-Accountant, adjusting his spectacles with administrative despair. "They came out of Slipwood Forest this morning and appear to have decided property values are better by the river. Which they are. But still, the proper way to acquire land is to purchase it and file the right forms." He looked quite vexed.

A poplar nudged a lamppost toward the river with an air of helpfulness. Another attempted to reverse, trod on its own roots, and collapsed into a shed.

"They're… arranging it," said Viola.

"With or without paperwork," Pall replied.

One poplar leaned into the bakery and delicately pushed the oven three feet left. The wall followed.

"Has anyone tried talking to them?" Viola asked.

The Mayor-Accountant consulted his notes. "Inconclusive: Old Mr. Churro shouted, 'Get off my lawn,' which they did—onto his house. Mrs. Soukville screamed about her flowerbeds—no effect. Tommy

Tinkleson threw stones and told them to bugger off. Swatted."

The fallen Gideon struggled to rise, crushing a shed. A smaller poplar stood beside it, trembling like a child. Viola stepped closer.

"Don't be afraid," she said. "I'm sure your mother—" She studied the fallen tree, "or father— is fine."

The big one managed to right itself, then slipped again and crashed down, snapping several branches. Viola winced.

The sapling turned toward its parent's sound.

Tim buzzed excitedly.

"Yes," Viola said, "it does seem to hear sound. But how do we talk to it?"

She tapped her foot, thinking. The sapling leaned closer, root-tips shifting in the soil.

"Uh, Viola?" Pall said. "Your foot. It's listening."

Indeed, it was. It had tilted, curious.

She tried different patterns and got different results. She would tap, and the sapling swayed. It wasn't so much talking as a sort of interpretive dance.

Another joined.

A third copied badly and corrected itself with an embarrassed rustle.

Soon a dozen thin trunks were rocking to Viola's various beats, branches waving in the air.

Meanwhile, however, the large trees continued to blunder around, breaking things. Viola stomped more vigorously on the ground. She asked Pall to help. Despite their efforts, the adult Gideons were too old or too large to hear them.

"It's not enough," she said. "We need everyone."

Within minutes half the town had gathered—some alarmed, some resigned, but all politely cooperative.

North of Sumpford lay a flat meadow by the river.

"What about there?" she said. "Plenty of room and already damp."

They began to jump in rhythm. It took practice, but soon the crowd managed:

STOMP STOMP – STOMP

STOMP STOMP – STOMP

The first great poplar followed. Root-tips lifted and set in cautious time. Houses scraped but did not break. Windows sighed as the light shifted off their faces.

They processed through Sumpford at the pace of a slow parade. Townsfolk lined the road, astonished into enthusiasm. Someone began clapping. The goose calmed. The march of Gideon Poplars passed with dignity.

"Left, left, right, pause," Viola called. "Mind the roots."

By late afternoon the trees had reached the meadow. The ground grew soft; several trees tangled; but finally a Gideon's root found the stream's edge and then, just like that, the whole pack was rushing to the water.

Well, "rushing" might be a bit of an exaggeration. They were trees, after all. Even so, their roots moved with purpose that would likely be considered a sprint in the world of trees. The parents would tell stories for years about the Great Race to the River.

Viola swept her umbrella wide. "This is yours," she told them.

The poplars hesitated, tasting earth and air with a million toes, then settled—roots sinking, leaves lifting. A hush fell that belonged to afternoons and bees.

The town exhaled.

Sumpford took stock. The bakery stood slightly diagonal but serviceable. The apothecary re-emerged. The mayor's office was discovered leaning against the pump and declared improved by it.

Already, several townsfolk were forming an informal working group to discuss what sort of committee ought to be established to study the day's events. Someone was drafting an agenda. Someone else was looking for chairs.

A deputation produced soup from what remained of their larders. Viola and Pall ate gratefully while Tim accepted a cube of cheese his own size and retired to enjoy it privately.

When the bowls were empty, Viola looked north. "We should go."

"Yes," said Pall. "Before someone asks us to chair a meeting."

They turned up the lane as the townsfolk began discussing where to re-put the statue. The road led them north past the meadow where the Gideon Poplars had settled by the water. As they passed, the trees rustled—in thanks, perhaps, or maybe it was just the wind.

Chapter 13

The rain gave up at the edge of the Slipwood Forest, as if even it preferred not to go in. The trees grew close and thoughtful, their trunks wrapped in moss thick enough to muffle footsteps. The air smelled of mushrooms, damp leaves, and quiet disagreement.

They folded their umbrellas and walked for some time without speaking. The forest had the kind of silence that suggested it was listening. When the light began to fade, they stopped beside a fallen tree whose bark had rotted into velvet.

Dinner was one crust of bread, two apples of doubtful character, and the merfolk's seaweed packets, still tied with bright ribbon. Tim inspected the contents, decided they were not leaves and therefore safe to eat, and began at once.

"It's lovely here," said Viola, gazing upward. "The air smells clean."

"I think that's decay," said Pall.

They ate in companionable resignation until something glimmered between the trees. At first it looked like fireflies—tiny lamps drifting in slow circles. Then the lights began to move together, like dancers finding the same tune. Gold, rose, and pale green shimmered through the branches.

"Oh," breathed Viola. "Beautiful."

Tim hopped down and began to follow, his antennae waving dreamily.

"Tim!" she called.

Pall caught him mid-hop, cupping him like a wayward firefly. "Don't look," he said. "Fairies. They're dangerous."

"How can they be dangerous?" Viola asked, puzzled. "They're just pretty lights."

From within the trees came a whispered sound that almost resembled laughter.

Pall shook his head. "Stare too long and they hypnotise you—like what happened to Tim. Then you wander off the path and vanish. They say the forest floor is littered with the bones of travellers who followed fairy lights."

Tim shook himself free of the cobwebs, vouched for the hypnosis with a few emphatic clicks, and tapped Pall's hand in thanks.

They moved on. The fairies stayed near, dancing in the shadows. Their laughter continued, though Viola could not tell whether it was playful or mocking.

The path narrowed, the light thinned, and the forest pressed close around them. The ordinary sounds of the woods seemed suddenly loud and deliberate.

Viola shivered. "It's getting cold."

Pall stopped and took stock. He shook his head as if to say *I knew this was a bad idea from the beginning.* Which, to be fair, he did.

"No flint. No steel. And no shelter. It's going to be a long, uncomfortable night—assuming we aren't eaten, which is not guaranteed."

He stooped, found a stick, and tested its weight. "At least now we have a weapon," he said.

Viola studied him. "You might manage to frighten a squirrel."

"I'm stronger than I look," he insisted. But he did convert it to a walking stick, which seemed to Viola far more practical.

Still, Pall was not content. He started muttering.

"What were we thinking?"

"We were thinking bravely," said Viola.

After a bit he declared, "I knew this was going to end badly."

"Then at least you can't be disappointed."

He wasn't calmed. "We're cold, and alone, and probably going to die here in this forest. Likely no one will find us until we're just bones."

Without thinking, she snapped back, "Then let's make our bones memorable—"

The words hung there. Viola's voice faltered. She saw his face close, the shadow under his collarbone where the hunch bent his shoulders. He looked away, and in that moment she understood exactly what she had said.

Her stomach turned to stone. "Oh—Pall, I didn't mean—"

He shook his head, quietly. "Doesn't matter."

But it did. His hands tightened on the walking stick until the wood creaked. "They already are memorable," he muttered. "For all the wrong reasons."

Viola's face burned. The apology stuck like a lump in her throat. She wanted to explain that she hadn't meant *his* bones—that she'd meant courage, or legacy, or something else entirely—but she knew that would only make it worse.

"I'm sorry," she said softly.

He said nothing.

They walked in silence. The fairies followed at a distance, their laughter dimming into a hiss.

Then Tim's tiny hand tapped anxiously at her neck, and she felt him go still. Something was watching them.

A small figure stood among the roots, motionless but unmistakably alive. She was about Viola's height—perhaps a little smaller—though thinner, as if carved from a single sapling and shaped, mostly, like a little girl.

As Viola stepped closer, the details emerged. Her skin was pale birch wood, fine-grained, with larger bark bits forming the impression of a short dress. No shoes. Just two thin legs with feet and longish root-like toes. Her hair hung in thin vines threaded with tiny leaves, and along her neck and shoulders small mushrooms grew like bits of jewellery. Her eyes, large and amber as drops of resin, caught the light without returning it.

It was, of course, a wood-elf—one of those half-tree, half-child creatures who grow where forests have been left to dream too long. They are said to live for centuries and to distrust all things made of meat. But this one seemed quite young and apparently didn't know she was supposed to stay away from humans. She regarded them calmly, not at all afraid.

Pall stepped protectively in the way, holding up his stick.

"Stop it," said Viola, pushing the stick down. Then to the elf: "Hello!"

The creature tipped her head and looked at them curiously. "What sort of creature are you?" she asked. Her voice was low and musical, like a bubbling brook.

"We're humans. Except for Tim. He's a locust."

"What's a human?"

Viola wasn't quite sure how to answer that. "Um… we're made of flesh and bones. And we live in cities."

"What's a city?"

At this point Viola realised two things: first, that the wood-elf was a child; and second, that they might be some time if every answer led to another question. So she tried a different approach.

"I'm Viola. This is Pall. And this is Tim. What's your name?"

"Aaiah."

"That's a pretty name."

Pall muttered, "That's not a name; that's a very quiet scream."

Viola ignored him. "Aaiah, are your parents nearby?"

The girl shook her head. "I was following my friends."

Pall and Tim looked around nervously.

"Who are your friends?" Viola asked.

"The fairies."

In the forest, they were still there—slipping through the trees, whispering their strange laughter.

"I see."

Having decided the wood-elf was a lost child, Viola straightened. "Aaiah, we should find your family. Where did you come from?"

The little girl pointed into the forest.

"Oh no. Absolutely not," objected Pall.

Even Tim seemed to think it a bad idea; he buzzed in alarm.

"She's lost. We can't just leave her."

"That's exactly what we can do," said Pall. "She's half-tree. She'll be fine."

But he hesitated, and Viola saw the doubt in his face.

"Come on," Viola said to the little elf. "Take my hand, and let's find them."

The wood-elf's hand was soft and delicate, and quite cold. They stepped off the path.

Pall stood frozen for a moment, then sighed deeply. "Why did I ever agree to this?" he muttered, and followed.

The path disappeared behind them almost at once, swallowed by shadow and undergrowth.

And gloom took them.

Chapter 14

he fairies would not go away.

They drifted beside them like scraps of coloured smoke, laughing as if someone had told them a scandal about humans. Tim kept going soft in the eyes and drifting toward them. Twice Pall caught him by the wings. The third time Pall said, "That's enough of that," and stuffed Tim into his coat pocket.

"It's safer," Pall said.

"For whom?" came Tim's muffled voice.

"For my nerves."

Tim rustled inside the pocket. He discovered a small rind of cheese and half a cracker. Both disappeared in his usual ravenous way of eating—followed, by accident, by a neat crescent of fabric that left a tiny hole like a window.

"My pocket!" Pall cried, clutching the wound.

A faint, unrepentant buzz answered him.

Off the path, the forest grew thick and opinionated. Branches leaned together as though sharing private remarks. Leaves trembled when no wind touched them, as if repeating gossip.

"Do you hear them?" Viola asked.

"Trees talk too slowly," said Aaiah. She pointed at a nearby oak. "I think that one is going to say *perhaps*, but she's only reached the *per* part."

"Perfect," said Pall glumly.

"Or that," Aaiah agreed. "Though things are rarely perfect for the trees."

A large boulder squatted ahead, the sort that made a statement about permanence. Viola looked at it, looked away, and looked back in time to see it settle half a step nearer, the way a tired person shifts their weight.

She decided not to mention it. Pall was upset enough.

The light thinned until it felt like breath on glass. The ground took an interest in tripping their feet. Pall sweated and worried—sometimes in that order, sometimes both at once.

Viola told herself they were fine until she stepped into a puddle with ambitions of being a pond. Cold water poured into her shoes and up her trousers to the knee.

"Oh," she said, and sat down hard.

When she stood again, her trousers were soaked and decorated with a rich brown that would not be fashionable anywhere. Worse, she had crushed the entrance to a bustling ant city. The ground hissed. Hundreds of ants boiled out—indignant, repairing, shouting, if one could shout in ant.

Tim shot out of the pocket like a cork and planted himself in the mud, gesturing furiously. His wings flicked; his antennae lashed. Whatever he said was sharp enough to make the lead ant rear back. The two of them faced each other like duelists waiting for the signal.

"Oh dear," said Viola. "Tim, it's not worth all that."

Aaiah watched, head tilted. Then, very calmly, she knelt and laid her small wooden hand upon the mud. Something in the ground seemed to exhale. The crushed dirt lifted and knit. A tiny arch formed; twig braces sprouted from nowhere; a sliver of bark slid into place like a door. It was not what the ants had before, but it was a house, and it stood.

The ants paused—even the angry one. Then he turned away and began barking orders at the swarm. Despite the improvement, they carried on fixing everything anyway, needing it exactly to their satisfaction.

If you are the sort of person who likes a home to stay the way you left it, do not marry an ant. Every day is a new home plan.

They walked on, wet and chastened.

Aaiah squeezed Viola's hand and, being a child, began to ask questions as children are wont to do.

"Why is your hand so warm?"

"Because there's blood inside," said Viola.

"What is blood?"

"A warm liquid that keeps us alive."

"Like sap?"

"Sort of," said Viola. "Only not as dignified."

"Do you have magic?"

"No."

"That is sad."

"Probably," Viola admitted. "But we make do."

Aaiah nodded at Viola's raincoat. "Why is your skin different colours?"

"Oh—that's clothing," said Viola, pulling the edge to show it wasn't attached.

Aaiah marvelled. "What's clothing?"

"It covers your body and keeps it warm. Though mine's not working very well at the moment," she added, shivering.

"Why not just grow clothing?"

"We can't do that, sweetie."

Aaiah thought about this as they trudged on. The forest did not seem to want them and kept laying branches and roots in their way.

"Is it fall where you come from?"

"No. It's summer. Same as here."

"Then where are your leaves?"

"We don't grow leaves."

"When was Tim born?"

"I don't know."

"Isn't he your sapling?"

"No. He's a locust."

Aaiah frowned, considering that.

"Where are you going?"

"To the sea," said Viola.

"What's that?"

"A large body of water."

"We have those here."

"Well, we need a much bigger one. One that goes on almost forever."

"Oh. Where is it?"

"We don't exactly know," said Pall. "Not that anyone's asked me."

Aaiah pointed in three possible directions.

By now it was very dark. The fairies, at last bored of being ignored, drifted off with a few tinkling notes of laughter. Silence fell.

The forest kept listening.

Viola's teeth began to chatter. She told them to stop, but they didn't listen.

"Here," Pall said, giving her his scarf. It wasn't warm, but it had the virtue of being dry—and therefore hopeful.

Pall, who by now had settled into a permanent state of dread, suggested they climb out of the dark of the forest.

"And find out exactly how lost we are," he said. "With luck."

The boulder's surface was slick and pitted like old bread. Viola went first because she was lighter. Pall followed, testing every handhold twice and sighing after each. Aaiah moved like a shadow, feet finding the places roots would choose. Tim peered out of Pall's pocket, buzzing instructions no one understood.

At the top, they could see over the close-packed crowns. The forest rolled away in every direction—a black-green sea with no waves and too many secrets. There were no lamps, no chimneys. The clouds had lowered until they seemed a roof.

Viola turned slowly. "Aaiah, can you see your home?"

The wood-elf's amber eyes shone like sap in moonlight. She looked for a long time, not sad, only exact.

"Maybe that tall one?" she said, pointing to a clump of trees in the distance, one dominated by a spectacularly tilted oak.

Pall made a small sound that might have been agreement or despair. "At least," he said, "we know we're lost everywhere at once."

Somewhere below, a sound rolled through the forest—a long howl, low and rising at the end like a question.

They froze.

It came again, closer this time. The trees seemed to draw together, listening too.

"What was that?" whispered Viola.

Pall swallowed. "Something hungry."

Aaiah tilted her head. "Hollowmanes."

They stood in the dark on the stone, listening. The sound came once more, deeper now, echoing through the trunks like breath in a hollow chest.

Tim's antennae trembled.

"Aaiah," Viola asked, "are hollowmanes friendly?"

Aaiah considered this. "Sometimes," she said. "But not usually."

Far below, the howl came again—long, deep, and searching.

Chapter 15

Viola reached out to Pall, and he held on to her as if he were drowning and she were a raft.

Tim pressed himself flat inside Pall's pocket, barely able to peer out his small window, antennae trembling like compass needles unsure of north.

The forest below them breathed, then held its breath again. Something moved among the trees—large enough to make the undergrowth whisper in alarm. The sound came once, then again, nearer.

Another cry rose—half howl, half question—and was answered by a second from deeper in the woods. The air thickened with listening.

Aaiah, pale and calm, tilted her head as though identifying the note. "More than one," she said, as if naming the weather.

"Splendid," Pall muttered. "At least we shall be eaten quickly. Hopefully?"

Branches cracked. Brush parted. Something pawed at the ground below, then sniffed—long, deliberate breaths that climbed upward through bark and rain-soaked air.

"Do we run?" Viola whispered.

Pall glanced at the sheer drop behind them. "Into the forest or into the sky?"

Neither seemed promising. A branch cracked again. Then another. The silence that followed was worse—alive, listening.

So they did nothing at all: just three silhouettes and a shivering pocket, waiting.

The sniffing came closer. Then a voice, low and liquid like water poured over stone, lifted up to them. "Aaiah?"

Aaiah cupped her small hands around her mouth. "I am up here!"

The reply was immediate—a rustle, a command, the thud of padded feet. From the gloom below emerged a company of shapes that caught what little light remained: slender figures, pale as birch bark, moving with the certainty of those who never trip over roots.

Wood-elves.

They rode up the stone on the backs of their hollowmane mounts— six in all—and dismounted before them. They were beautiful in the way storms are: fascinating, but best admired from shelter. Faces like carved ivory, eyes like sap amber, garments woven of leaf-fibre and caught light.

Their beasts were enormous—wolf-shaped but stranger—dark as shadow, with manes like wind-tossed smoke and eyes burning yellow with malice. Their paws were the size of soup plates. Saddles of woven bark and bronze clung to their backs, suggesting both intelligence and terrible obedience.

Viola gripped Pall's sleeve. "They ride them?"

"Of course," said Aaiah. "When you need to go fast, there is nothing faster on the ground."

The largest hollowmane bared its teeth in what might have been a grin, revealing a cruel line of razors. It did little to calm their nerves.

Aaiah toddled forward along the rock and was immediately scooped into the arms of one of the elves—a woman whose hair fell in silver threads. A male laid a hand on Aaiah's head and inspected her as though counting the number of splinters.

"She is unharmed," said the mother. Her voice was soft but carried the weight of command.

To Aaiah she said, "What were you thinking?"

A human mother, having found her lost child, might have mixed relief with anger. Not so the elves. The question was purely factual, without the slightest bite.

Aaiah looked up at her and answered in kind. "The fairies said they had some fun and wished to show me."

"Have we not told you never to listen to fairies?" asked the father.

"Yes," she said, nodding. "But I wanted fun."

Until now, the elves had paid no attention to Viola and Pall. Their eyes turned at last toward the frightened youths.

"Humans," growled the nearest hollowmane, sniffing.

Aaiah pointed back at them. "They helped me not die."

"That is specific," Pall murmured.

The elves regarded the humans without expression. Their eyes moved slowly, as if light travelled through them at a different speed. Behind them, the hollowmanes shifted, claws scraping stone.

"Best to kill them," rumbled the lead beast. "Humans travel in packs and bring fire."

The elves listened. The mother turned slightly toward it.

Viola blinked. "Oh. That really isn't necessary."

Pall fell to his knees before the elves. "Please! We don't have any packs or any fire! I don't want to die!"

The elves conferred in low tones, precise and unhurried, like scholars debating a footnote. The hollowmanes growled again, offended by moderation. Finally, the mother raised a hand.

"No," she said. "They are of rain, not fire."

The beasts settled back on their haunches, eyes on their masters as though awaiting permission for the matter to be reconsidered.

Aaiah wriggled free and gestured toward her companions. "This one is Viola. This one is Pall. And the one in the pocket is Tim. He eats cloth."

There was a pause.

The male inclined his head a fraction. "Welcome to Slipwood, human-folk. You are a long way from home."

Viola managed a curtsy. "Thank you for not letting us be eaten."

Tim buzzed nervously. Pall got back to his feet and tried to stay as far as possible from any teeth.

The mother regarded them all. "You will come with us," she said. "The forest is restless tonight."

One of the great beasts sighed, evidently disappointed to be denied a hot meal.

Aaiah took Viola's hand again, at ease among her towering kin. "See? I told you they were sometimes friendly."

Chapter 16

ollowmanes run like thunder given legs—if thunder had decided to take up running and enjoyed dodging around trees. Viola and Pall were seated before their riders, small bundles strapped into the saddles as the forest blurred past. The air rushed cold and sharp, tossing their hair as if it enjoyed swatting them.

Viola laughed, wind-struck and giddy.

Pall clung to the pommel with both hands, repeatedly saying, "We're going to die," which only made his mount snort and run faster.

The riders said nothing. Wood-elves, Viola had learned, spoke only when silence wouldn't do the job for them.

They rode down unknown paths, deeper into the forest. The land fell away, and the trees grew larger, until they towered around them like cathedrals. Green light and mist poured out from hidden cracks, turning the world to green mist and magic. Once, Viola caught a glimpse of something watching from the

branches—a creature made of bark and amber eyes—
but it vanished before she could be sure it had been
there.

Then at last the trees fell away entirely, and before
them rose the Great Oak.

Viola's mouth fell open.

Pall made a small sound that might have been awe—
or sickness from the ride.

It was less a tree than a village. The trunk spread wider
than a barn; its roots gripped the earth like giant
fingers refusing to let go. Bridges, walkways, and
platforms of living wood stuck out from its sides,
curved and alive, as if grown rather than built. Orbs
of soft gold hung glimmering among the leaves,
enchanted with forest magic. They turned every
raindrop into a star and every star into a small promise
that the world might, occasionally, be beautiful on
purpose.

Guards waited at the gate, slender figures with bows
and spears that looked grown rather than forged.
Their faces were smooth and ageless, as though they
remembered when your great-grandmother was
young and badly behaved. They nodded once, a
gesture that contained both welcome and warning,
and the riders passed through.

A spiral stair wound around the trunk, its railings
carved with beasts, leaves, and something that might
have been stories. Viola stared until her neck hurt. Pall

studied his hands, as they seemed much safer than the world around them.

The hollowmanes bounded up the stairs. Their claws gripped bark as if gravity meant nothing. Viola clutched the saddle and tried to remember how to breathe without screaming.

At last they stopped on a broad platform that jutted from the trunk like a balcony. The elves dismounted with the grace of people who had never fallen and didn't intend to start. They lifted Viola and Pall after them, setting them down as gently as if they were made of butterfly wings.

The beasts bowed their heads, a gesture of surprising courtesy from creatures that looked like they could snap bone without effort. Most vanished into the dark wood, silent as fog—except one, the great scarred creature that had smiled earlier. It settled beside the platform and lay, eyes closed, but still somehow looking like it might strike and devour them at any moment.

Aaiah went and hugged it, and the hollowmane's tail twitched once, lazily, like a cat.

"Fang likes you," she said to Viola.

"How can you tell?"

"It didn't eat you."

There were no walls and few ceilings, only branches and woven leaves. Where the forest trees had seemed to whisper about them, the Great Oak felt alive and watching, as if each branch were a separate granny, and they all had opinions about you.

Somewhere, someone played a flute—and the melody danced in the air, like water running over stones, or perhaps stones dancing in the water.

Viola leaned on the railing, dizzy with height and wonder. The ground was so far below it was lost from sight. Birds flew beneath her feet. The wind smelled of pine and black tea with a faint hint of honey.

Pall stayed back, eyeing the drop as if it might jump out and grab him. His knuckles were white on his walking stick.

"It's safe," said a young elf with hair like autumn and a mouth like a knife kept sharp for special occasions.

"I'll take your word for it," Pall said, not moving.

Aaiah stretched. "I'm hungry."

Viola's stomach answered before she could, a low growl of agreement.

So they were led to dinner.

The hall was open to the air on three sides, its ceiling a lattice of branches. Somehow, the sky above them held no clouds, and stars peered down like curious neighbours. A table of polished bark ran down the centre, broad enough for twenty. Elves came and went—some young, some ancient—all helping themselves as they needed. They studied the humans with curiosity mixed with the patience of people who had outlived urgency.

Aaiah tugged Viola toward a table already laid with small dishes. "Try this!" she declared, and proceeded to introduce Viola to everything.

The food was strange and wonderful: moss that tasted of honey and earth, shining fungi that glowed faintly on the tongue, roasted nuts that cracked like tiny thunder, and bowls of clear water that tasted faintly of lightning—sharp, bright, impossibly clean. There were berries that changed flavour with every bite, bread woven rather than baked, and a stew of roots and wild herbs that tasted like every autumn at once.

Pall eyed his bowl. "I'm not one for odd food," he said. "But the stew's decent. Could use a little lamb. Or fish."

The silver-haired wood-elf turned her gaze on him, calm as moonlight. "If you like flesh, you may dine with the hollowmanes. They brought down a stag this morning."

Pall froze. "That's… thoughtful. But I think I'll stick with plants."

The father's mouth twitched, which might have been amusement, though it was hard to tell. The elves did not laugh or play. They were always calm and matter-of-fact, except Aaiah, of course, on account of her young age.

Aaiah's mother looked back to Viola. "Does the food suit you, human child?"

"Oh, yes," said Viola, quite earnest. "It's the best meal I've ever eaten, and possibly the best anyone has ever eaten in the history of the world."

The father inclined his head. "Few speak so well of moss and water."

Viola hesitated, then smiled. "It must be the seasoning."

Aaiah laughed, delighted. "That's my father's magic. It's sprinkled with tree mana."

Viola smiled. She turned to Aaiah's parents. "I'm sorry. I want to thank you for your kindness, but I don't know your names."

The father straightened slightly. "I am Ael," he said. "This is Her Highness, Queen Isiiala of Slipwood."

Pall coughed into his bowl.

Viola's spoon paused midway to her mouth. She tried to stand and curtsey, but ended up tripping and falling over instead.

"I'm so sorry. Your Majesties. I didn't know—"

Ael reached out, lifted Viola effortlessly, and placed her back on her feet. "Not majesties. Elves do not have kings."

Viola tried again. "Your Majesty," she said, curtseying.

Pall started to rise as well, to bow, but the Queen waved him down.

"Tonight, we are simply hosts."

"Hosts with very tall ceilings," Viola murmured, curtseying anyway.

"Please sit," continued the Queen. "And tell us your tale. The wind whispers around you, and I would know why."

Viola looked at Pall.

He sighed. "You start. I'll interrupt as needed."

"Well," she began, "it started when the boggarts moved into the moat at Dropminster."

"Uninvited," Pall added.

Viola considered. "Yes. Well. They were refugees from Crackendor, the country to the west of Dampenia. Apparently, someone smashed a statue, and suddenly everyone started smashing everything, including the boggarts' homes. So they ran east."

"And found our moat," Pall added.

Queen Isiiala raised an eyebrow. "Your king allowed them to stay?"

"Not exactly," said Viola. "King Darius did suggest they leave."

"They said no," said Pall.

"Yes. But, to be fair, they did say no politely," Viola added. "So that's something."

A few elves exchanged looks.

"Then came the merfolk," Viola continued. "They'd been driven from the Fae Isles by the Malogrodians—"

"Molgorodians," Pall corrected.

"Right. The Molgorodians took all the islands, which was awful, so the merfolk came ashore. They mean well but tend to make messes and not clean up. Also, they ate most of the fish."

"Merfolk," murmured an elf. "They care for nothing but their appearance."

Viola didn't want to say anything mean, but that was about right. So she just said, "Still, no one wanted to be rude, so nothing was done."

"And then," Pall said, "the locusts arrived."

"The Brean," Viola explained quickly. "The Czar of Molgorod decided they were pests and ordered them destroyed."

"They are pests," said Ael.

Tim buzzed indignantly.

"Even if they are," Viola responded—and then quickly added, "Not you, Tim," before continuing, "destroying a whole people doesn't seem right."

Tim rustled in agreement.

Pall picked up the thread. "So, of course, they flee to Dampenia, and they proceed to eat nearly everything—especially the pricklepepper."

Viola nodded. "Which is dreadful, because spicy soup is the heart of our people."

Queen Isiiala inclined her head. "What is your king doing to protect his people?"

"He formed a committee," answered Pall.

"A committee."

Pall waved a lazy hand. "They meet weekly to workshop a motion to do something. But the something isn't yet clear." Then, for clarity, he added, "It's mostly hopeless."

Ael nodded. "The sad human's assessment sounds accurate."

"Thank you," said Pall.

"So," said Viola, "since no one was actually doing anything, I thought maybe I could. I just want to talk to the Queen of the Brean. Maybe she's lonely, or frightened, or confused. Tim's one of them. He can translate."

Tim hopped out and gave a little bow.

Queen Isiiala studied them. "You plan to speak with the queen of locusts?"

"Yes," Viola said earnestly. "Someone has to."

Pall muttered, "The part where we get eaten seems under-discussed."

"Your intentions may be admirable, but your plan is foolish," said Queen Isiiala.

Viola shook her head. "I don't believe they are bad. Most folks aren't if you give them a chance. Maybe we can—I don't know—negotiate?"

"Negotiate with a locust," the Queen repeated. Her smooth face wrinkled slightly, as if the words tasted bitter.

"With a queen," Viola said. "That's why we came to your forest. The merfolk told us she lives in the Sea of Flumes—in the Mouth of Doom."

Those elves who had been listening stilled. Soft laughter rustled through the leaves—not unkind, but not quite kind either. It was the sound of people who had heard this story before and knew how it ended.

"A myth," said Ael. "The Mouth of Doom is real—a great whirlpool at the edge of the Flumes where the water falls into darkness. But no locust sits at its heart. No throne, no palace. Only water, and the things that live in water, and the things that used to."

"But the merfolk said—"

"Merfolk are liars."

Viola bristled. "They didn't seem like liars. They were—grand."

"Yes," said Ael. "That's how you know."

A younger elf with a crack like a scar down the side of his face leaned forward. "Whether they lie to others or to themselves, it amounts to the same. The merfolk live in memory. They see the world as it was, or as they wish it was, not as it is."

"But surely there is a queen, somewhere?" Viola asked, hope flickering like a candle refusing to go out.

"Oh yes," said Queen Isiiala. "But she rules underground. The Brean build palaces beneath the roots of the world—tunnels, nurseries, throne rooms carved from the earth. Her seat is there, in the dark, where the roots grow deep."

"Where?" Pall asked in a tone that said: *probably someplace worse.*

"Not in our kingdom, thankfully," said Queen Isiiala. "The Brean are many, but their queen is singular. She stays below. The others"—the Queen gestured vaguely—"are workers, soldiers, the mindless many. They follow instinct, not orders."

Pall's jaw tightened. "If someone—if we—killed her, would that stop the locusts?"

The hall went still.

The Queen's mouth was thin as bark, sad as winter. "If only. Queens die. Hunger does not."

The words hung in the air, heavy and true.

"Another queen rises," said the scarred elf. "Or the swarm fractures—ten thousand small hungers instead of one great one. Either way, they eat."

Viola felt something sink inside her. "So there's nothing we can do?"

The Queen regarded her, weighing something unseen. "I did not say that. But what you seek is not a simple answer. You wish to speak to their queen? Very well. Do not imagine that words will fill an empty belly, child. The Brean have eaten kingdoms before. They will eat kingdoms again."

"Then what do I do?"

Queen Isiiala regarded Viola with her deep, far-seeing eyes. "What heroes always do. Something very foolish, very brave—and hope the difference doesn't matter."

Somewhere in the darkness, Fang chuffed softly—a sound like laughter from something that knew better but approved anyway.

Chapter 17

They spent the night among the wood-elves, in the hollows of the Great Oak where the air smelled of sap and old magic. Viola, Pall, and Tim were given a bed of moss that glowed faintly from the roots beneath. There were no covers, but they didn't need any—the moss was warm to the touch. By some forest enchantment, the sky above remained clear of rain.

Tim, who had gorged himself on elvish sweets, fell promptly asleep, snoring with a faint buzz.

"This is like the most wonderful dream," Viola said, gazing at the stars.

"I hope I'm not allergic," said Pall, poking the moss.

"Do you think the elves are right? About the Queen of the Brean?"

"Well," Pall considered, "it's probably unwise to trust either of them. But I prefer not sailing to a watery doom."

"Oh, Pall," said Viola, "when will you stop finding the worst in everything?"

"I thought I was being positive."

Viola sighed. She looked at a twinkling star and wished that one day Pall would say something cheerful—and surprise himself by meaning it.

They laid their clothes aside and put on the shifts the Queen had made for them. They were woven of leaves but felt like silk. Viola fell asleep wrapped in the soft rustle of the forest.

In the morning they rose refreshed. Their clothes lay stacked at the foot of the bed, washed, pressed, and faintly scented of crabapples and roses.

An elf came to lead them back to the platform where they had first arrived. Queen Isiiala, Ael, and Aaiah stood waiting at the edge, still as statues, dappled in sunlight. The Queen had changed out of her riding bark into a gown of living wood that shimmered like wet leaves touched with gold. Her crown of foliage caught the dawn.

"You slept?" she asked.

"Oh yes, Your Majesty," said Viola. "I've never slept in so soft a bed. Thank you."

"Do you not sleep?" Pall asked.

"We do, when young—like Aaiah—but it fades with age." She brushed her daughter's cheek, and Aaiah's eyes fluttered open. Seeing Viola and Pall, she smiled.

A light breakfast was brought for them.

"Eat," said Ael. "Flesh needs fuel, and you have far to go."

At his words, the elves gathered silently around them.

"The Queen of the Locusts lies east," said Isiiala. Her voice was gentler now, but no less commanding. "Fang will carry you as far as the Underhills. From there, go to the burrows of the Talpan. Their king knows all the dark ways beneath the earth. He may guide you further."

At her gesture, Fang padded forward. In daylight his size was astonishing—sleek, fanged, and faintly luminous, as though carved from shadow and moonlight. When he opened his mouth in what might have been a grin, both children stepped back.

Pall whispered, "We'll be eaten before lunch."

Fang's ears twitched. "I heard that," he rumbled.

"Sorry," said Viola quickly. "Pall didn't mean it. I'm sure you're a complete gentleman."

Fang narrowed his molten eyes. "I am no man." His tail lashed. "And not gentle."

Too late, Viola realised both suggestions would be deeply insulting to a hollowmane.

"Of course," said Viola. "I meant—I'm sure you will protect us, and not harm us."

"I'll carry you because the Queen wishes it. As for protection—even pups learn to grow teeth or be eaten."

Queen Isiiala raised one pale hand. "Forgive them. They are only human."

"I am trying," Fang growled, with what might have been a sigh.

To mark their departure, the elves brought gifts.

Ael offered Pall a rapier of living wood, its guard curling in intricate loops of a duelist's blade. "For bravery," he said.

Pall took it awkwardly. "Bravery?" he muttered, looking at the weapon as though it had made a mistake.

An elder stepped forward with a slender staff of living wood. Buds tipped its length, tight as fists. "For the road," she said. "It will grow with you."

An old elf crone bent like a willow slid to Tim and presented a coil of thread, fine as spider silk yet impossibly strong. "For weaving," she said. "A better future, perhaps."

Tim removed his hat and bowed low.

Then the scarred elf approached Viola and placed in her arms a small vest. It was as supple as leather yet strong as armour. "Protect your greatest gift," he said, resting a hand lightly over her heart.

Aaiah stepped forward last and held out a bracelet of flowers crowned with a single red rose, bright as blood. "I made it myself," she said proudly.

"Thank you. It's beautiful."

Aaiah leaned close. "The fairies did not lie," she whispered. "I had fun."

"So did I," said Viola, and hugged her. Aaiah looked startled, then smiled.

Fang knelt, vast and patient. The elves provided them with elven-made packs to carry their things— beautifully woven of leaves and spider silk— tucking away umbrellas, food,  and flasks of elven water. Viola put on her vest and drew her raincoat over it. It made her feel brave and steady.

When all was ready, Viola climbed up, Pall after her, and Tim settled in Pall's pocket.

Queen Isiiala lifted her hand. "Go east. And remember—what grows in darkness may still seek the sun."

Fang snorted, scattering leaves. "Hold on," he said, and sprang forward.

They raced down the spiral stair and vanished into the mist. Behind them, the Great Oak creaked its farewell—a deep sound that seemed to fuss about dressing sensibly for adventures.

Chapter 18

Fang ran for hours, silent as shadow. The forest rolled beneath him like a dark sea, the children clinging to his back as if to a raft. Riding a hollowmane was rather like sitting atop a galloping thundercloud—thrilling, magnificent, and certain to make one's stomach regret being attached. The trees streamed past in green and gold ribbons, and the ground blurred into rhythm—thud, thud, thud—until even fear gave up trying to keep pace.

Once or twice, Viola dared to look up. The world tilted wildly around her—branches flashing overhead, wind biting her cheeks, Pall's hand clenched white on Fang's fur. They had ridden for so long her thoughts had become half-dreams: rain, breath, heartbeat, and the steady drumming of paws.

When at last Fang slowed, the air changed. The trees thinned. Ahead lay open country—vast, pale, and wind-torn. They had travelled dozens of leagues, though the children only knew this by how far away the forest now looked, and by how reluctant their legs were to stand.

The ground sloped into hills tufted with heather and stone. Rain clouds gathered above, patient as shepherds waiting for foolish sheep. Fang stopped at the edge of the shadowed wood and crouched.

"This," he said, "is as far as I go."

They slid from his back, wobbling. After so long astride him, the earth itself seemed to sway. Viola knelt and pressed her palm to the wet soil. It felt honest—ordinary, and gloriously still.

"Where are we?" she asked.

"The eastern edge of the Queen's realm," Fang said. "This is wild land, far from the eyes of humans. Stay in the shadows. Dangerous things live here."

"The Underhills," Pall murmured, squinting at the iron-coloured hills. "Far from safety."

"At least it's raining again," said Viola. The rain was the only thing familiar, and a comfort.

Fang flicked his tail. "The Talpan dwell east. You will find a great cleft in the rock and a broad track descending. Follow it."

"And the Talpan themselves?"

"A blind and fearful race," said Fang. "Growl often so they know you're not food. I would tell you to tread heavy, but you already do."

Pall studied his feet. "I'm not sure I can do this."

"Then do not waste the Queen's gifts," Fang said.

Viola took Pall's hand. "Come on. East."

The rain thickened, whispering against their coats.

The path rose steeply into a maze of boulders. The umbrellas stayed in their packs, as they often needed both hands to climb. Great stones jutted from the ground as if giants had been playing a game of *smash-the-hill* and lost interest halfway through. At first they crept from one to another, trying to stay unseen, but creeping always led to the hardest ground. Rivulets ran between the stones, turning the earth to brown soap. Pall slipped three times before Viola admitted that the forest had not taught her much about climbing.

Tim finally leapt down, gave a reproachful buzz, and hopped ahead to scout. Directly east rose a cruel tangle of stone. South-east looked gentler—green with grass and rolling slopes. Tim chose that way.

"We'll be in the open," Pall warned.

Tim pointed first to the hard way, shook his head, then to the easy way and hopped.

The easy way did look much better.

"Well," said Viola, "my clothes were so nice this morning. I hate to ruin them. Let's take the easy bit first and swing back after."

The easier bit proved delightfully easy. They made better time, and soon Viola began to hum. A walking tune came to her mind, and she shared it with the drizzle.

By midday they reached a high ridge. Below stretched the whole northern world: the Sea of Flumes glimmered like beaten tin, and the hills rolled southward like petrified waves.

Pall shaded his eyes. Overhead, a dark shape wheeled—wings too wide for a bird, tail too long for comfort.

"Maybe a giant bat?" said Viola.

"Whatever it is," Pall breathed, "it's seen us."

It descended swiftly, and the closer it came, the larger it grew. It had a serpent's head, vast bat wings with claws at the joints, powerful hind legs with more claws, and a long spiked tail. Its eyes were red—and hungry.

Too late, they started to run.

As you may have noticed, our heroes had taken the scenic route instead of following Fang's advice—and in

doing so had caught the attention of a mountain wyrm.

Wyrms come in all shapes and unpleasant habits. They prefer cruel climates, partly because they are cruel themselves. They eat meat—preferably alive, preferably screaming—and differ only in how they prepare it. Some roast, some dissolve, and a few rare varieties electrocute. All share teeth like carving knives and personalities to match.

This one was small by wyrm standards—ten feet long—but amply equipped to eat two children and a locust, and still have room for dessert.

They had not reached the nearest boulder before it landed in front of them. Its eyes glowed with savage hunger. Viola understood, suddenly, that not every creature wished to be understood. Some simply *were* terrible, and content to stay so.

Her mouth opened, but only a scream came out.

Pall stepped in front of her, shaking so hard the sword rattled in his hands. "Back!" he shouted. "Back!"

As battle cries go, it was not distinguished. But it was, at least, sincere.

He thrust with both hands. The point of the sword bounced off its scaled hide with a spark.

The wyrm hissed and flared its wings. Its muscles bunched to leap upon them.

Viola thought, *Well, this is it. Pall was right after all.*

Then the hillside exploded.

A black blur of teeth and fury struck the wyrm side-on. Fang had returned. He caught it by the neck and hurled it against the stones. The struggle was terrible: claws against fangs, shadow against scale. When it ended, the wyrm was very still, and Fang was bleeding but alive.

"You fools," Fang growled, panting. "I told you to stay out of sight."

Viola knelt beside him, rummaging in their packs. "Oh, Fang—your paw! Hold still."

He snarled but did not bite. "You're lucky I smelled the wyrm and assumed you'd do something foolish."

Pall eyed the corpse. "Is *that* what it is?" He shuddered. "I never imagined the world had such terrible things."

"It does. And worse," said Fang.

"Thank you," Viola said quietly. "We'd be dead if not for you."

"Yes," he said. "You would."

"Is there anything we can do to help?"

He hesitated, pride wrestling pain. "Elf-water. On the cloth."

Pall handed her the small pouch. Viola soaked a rag and pressed it to the wound. The bleeding stopped.

"My gosh," she whispered.

"Don't waste it," Fang muttered.

She worked carefully until the worst gashes closed. Fang rose stiffly, shook out his fur, and limped toward the slope.

"Enough," he said. "Let's reach the burrow before you find another way to get me killed."

Chapter 19

he burrow of the Talpan King lay hidden in a cleft between two steep hills. The cliffs leaned close, as if conspiring to keep the secret.

Fang halted where a wide, scraped track led down into shadow. He sniffed once, then snorted.

"They are listening," he said, "but too afraid to come out."

Viola looked up at him. "Will you be all right?"

His ears flattened. "I am not a pet."

She meant to hug him but thought better of it. "Thanks," she said instead. The word felt small.

Fang turned to Pall. "You struck the wyrm. That is a start."

"I hope there won't be a next time," said Pall. "I'm not made for bravery."

"No one is," said Fang. "Next time, look for your enemy's weakness—the neck, the underbelly. Make fear your weapon."

Viola peered into the dark gorge. "Are you sure you can't come with us? What if we need you?"

He sighed, long and smoky. "You are worse than cubs. There's a whistle in the pack by my neck. Take it—it belonged to the princess, so don't lose it."

She found it: a carved piece of wood, smooth and beautiful.

"It's not my quest," Fang said. "And I couldn't care less about humans. Don't call me unless you are actually dying."

Then he was gone, melting into the rain.

Pall exhaled. "That may be some of the worst advice ever."

Viola brushed her coat, tucked the whistle into a pocket, and fixed her hair. "Let's just hope the Talpan are kind."

"In comparison," said Pall, "anything would be."

"Fang is kind," she said. "He's just stern."

"And a killer."

"And a good thing too," she said, remembering the wyrm.

Tim, who had been listening, buzzed in agreement.

They started down the broad track. The darkness rose around them, damp and deep. Remembering Fang's warning that the Talpan were a blind and fearful race, they walked loudly.

"Hello?" called Viola.

"Hello?" echoed Pall.

The light thinned to nothing. They began to wish for a lantern.

"Hello?"

"Shhh." The reply came from somewhere ahead—a low, nasal voice, as though the speaker were talking through a cold. "No need to shout."

"Sorry," said Viola. "We're looking for the Talpan."

"What's looking?" asked a second, higher voice with the same nasal twang.

The creatures hiding in the dark were Talpan moles—large, nearly hairless beings roughly the size of small bears, who lived their entire lives underground. Their claws were long and hard, shaped for digging, and their eyes so small as to be ornamental. They were famous for their tunnels, their temper, and their complete disregard for sunlight. Looking was not a word they understood. They knew *see* and *eyes*, but both referred to an impractical hobby of surface-dwellers.

Viola hesitated. It was a difficult question.

"Two humans and a locust," said Pall helpfully.

Whispers followed.

"We don't want any," said the low voice.

"I'm sorry," said Viola, "but we can't see you. Could you come out? It's rather hard to talk when you can't see who you're talking to."

"We are out," came the low voice.

"And you don't need to see to talk," said the high one. "You need to see to see."

"Still," Viola said gently, "would you be so kind? I'd just like to know to whom I'm speaking."

More whispering.

"I'm Guardmole Humhum," said the first.

"And I'm Guardmole Numni," said the second.

"Well, Humhum and Numni," said Viola, "if you won't come out of the dark, may we come in?"

Whispers again, then: "Suit yourself."

Viola stepped forward, hand outstretched, the way one does when entering a dark room. She couldn't see a thing. Pall followed, trembling but trying to be brave, sword pointed ahead.

Tim, who could see perfectly, buzzed furious directions—but as no one understood Locus, his advice (which was excellent) went entirely unheeded.

"Ow!" cried Numni, who had just been poked. "What did you do that for?"

"Sorry," said Pall. "I can't see a thing."

"Of course you can't see a thing! You're underground, where it's safe and nice."

"Not nice for us. We don't like the dark."

"Don't like the dark? Whoever heard of such a thing! And even if you are, that's no excuse for poking people with pointy sticks."

"I said I was sorry."

"Then how did the pointy part end up in front of you?"

Viola raised her voice. "Please—no one wants to hurt anyone. We only wish to speak with the King of the Talpan."

"Absolutely not," said Humhum. "We're guards. We keep people out. That's our job."

"Surely there are times you have guests?"

A pause.

"Well… yes," admitted Numni. "But the King is very busy."

"And besides," added Humhum, "we don't want your kinds."

Viola was shocked. "But we've done nothing to you."

"Yes you have." A large finger tapped her elven vest. "You humans gave the orders, and he"—there was a swish of air toward Tim—"started filling our barrows and eating everything. Now our children are hungry."

"That wasn't us," said Viola. "That's why we're here. Even Tim. We're trying to stop the plague of locusts that's eating everything. Queen Isiiala of the wood-elves sent us to you. Please don't send us away. We've come ever so far."

At the Queen's name the guards fell silent.

"Trying to help?" Numni repeated, doubtful.

"Yes," said Viola. "Truly."

The moles shuffled off into the dark.

"Wait here," said Humhum.

They heard the scrape of a heavy door opening, then closing with a thud. The tunnel was quiet again, filled only with the slow, patient breathing of the earth.

Time passed—so long, in fact, that they began to think they'd been forgotten. Their eyes adjusted little by little, enough to tell shadow from deeper shadow.

But they had not been forgotten. Just as hope was beginning to fade, the great door creaked open and the guards returned.

"You will come with us."

Viola stepped forward and promptly collided with Humhum, landing with a bump. "Ow."

Strong paws lifted her upright. "Do you not know how to travel together?" he asked.

"I suspect not," she admitted.

He placed her hand on his back. It was surprisingly soft. "When underground," he explained, "you must touch each other. Otherwise, everyone would be bumping into everyone all the time."

"Am I supposed to touch you too?" came Pall's voice from the dark.

"Of course," said Numni. "And put that sword away."

"I said sorry…"

So, connected by touch to their guides, they made their slow and careful way into the barrow.

Chapter 20

The darkness was the sort that made you doubt your eyes were open. Viola blinked several times to check. They were. It didn't help.

The Talpan took their barrows seriously. They smoothed the dirt floors until they were as neat as carpet. They carved rooms that sloped gently into one another, like a very organized anthill designed by someone with opinions about interior flow.

The air smelled strongly of earth—the good sort, like a garden after rain—though Viola suspected that was simply what underground smelled like when one lived in it on purpose.

Humhum led the way, tugging her gently by the hand on his back. Numni guided Pall. Tim clung to Viola's shoulder, his tiny locust feet gripping her collar.

"Try not to breathe on me," Numni muttered.

"I'm not breathing on you," Pall protested. "I'm just breathing near you. It's unavoidable."

"Well, avoid it anyway."

Every so often they passed other Talpan working in the dark—or at least Viola assumed they were, judging by the small shuffling sounds and the occasional clink of tools. Conversations stopped as they approached. There was sniffing. Whispers. The vague sense of shapes moving aside, like shadows rearranging themselves.

"Humans and a locust in the barrow?" someone muttered. "What is the world coming to?"

"We told them to go, but they wouldn't," Numni said loudly, as though that explained everything.

The response was a deeply unimpressed hmph, followed by the sound of someone flouncing away. Viola hadn't known one could flounce without being seen, but apparently it was possible.

"Very improper," another voice added.

"We're just following orders," Humhum said, a little defensively.

Somewhere behind them a whisper asked, "What is he thinking?"

"Mad, I tell you," came the reply.

Who *he* was remained unclear, though Viola suspected it meant the King. She hoped it was only an expression; persuading a sane monarch was already difficult enough.

"We'd better not get demoted because of you," Numni snapped.

"You haven't done anything wrong," Viola said, trying to be kind.

"Says you."

Fortunately, barrows have no stairs. Everything sloped—gently up, gently down—one room flowing into the next like a conversation that had forgotten where it started. Viola found it quite pleasant, aside from the complete absence of light.

They turned a corner, and the air began to change. It felt larger somehow, less close. The smell of earth faded, replaced by the cool openness of a wider space.

Then, from ahead: "Halt! Who goes there?"

Humhum sighed. "Come on, Duurgr. We were just here."

"Protocol is a matter of importance!" Duurgr announced. Then, in a loud whisper that defeated the point of whispering: "That's the difference between Burrow Guard and King's Guard." A deep breath followed, as if he were puffing out his chest.

"You're not a King's Guard," Numni retorted. "You're a *part-time junior* King's Guard."

"Oh! You haven't heard?"

There was shuffling. Something was passed forward. Humhum touched it.

"He's got the Wompol Stick," he reported, sounding resigned.

Duurgr preened audibly. "Full-time junior King's Guard. His Royal Highness granted me the honour today, recognizing my years of excellent service."

There was a pause while everyone absorbed this.

Humhum, to his credit, accepted the new reality. "Burrow Guards Humhum and Numni, presenting respectfully, requesting an audience with His High Most Excellent and Rotund Lordship."

Silence. Then the sound of scribbling in the dark. Evidently Duurgr was taking notes.

"And when would that be for?" he asked.

"Today, if possible," Humhum replied.

More scribbling.

"And who should, um, advance your request to His Lordship, may I note?"

"If the King's Guard would allow it," said Numni through gritted teeth.

Duurgr made considering noises—small hums and thoughtful grunts, like someone deciding which cheese to buy. "He's quite busy today," he said at last.

Numni exploded. "He just commanded us to get the humans!"

"Well… that was some time ago."

"It was an hour!"

"I will need to consult. Remain here."

A door closed.

"Ohhh, there'll be no living with him now," Numni fumed. "What was the King thinking? The most pompous, insufferable—"

"Now, now." Humhum patted her gently.

"And now we're stuck with these humans. And a locust! I may never get the stink off my skin."

"That's mean," Pall said. "It's not like we're right here able to hear you."

"Well, how would you like it if I were pawing you?"

Viola intervened before tempers worsened. "I'm sure you're doing a very good service to your country. Maybe the King will recognize your sacrifice."

She felt Humhum's head turn toward her. "Oh. Do you think so?"

"Well, some might consider it brave—escorting another species."

Humhum liked that. "That's true."

Then, in a moment of inspiration, Viola added, "Perhaps it could even lead to a promotion?"

That did it. All thought of the unpleasantness of humans—and even locusts—vanished.

"Get your hand back on me, human," Numni ordered Pall, who had clearly dropped it. "The King needs to be impressed with our quality."

"Quite right," Humhum agreed.

The door reopened. Duurgr emerged, sounding pleased with himself. "As it happens, I was able to squeeze you in. The King will accept you now."

They passed through the door into an even larger chamber. The air felt vast—cathedral-sized, though Viola still couldn't see a thing. The ground beneath their feet changed from packed earth to smooth stone. Their shuffling footsteps echoed.

At last, they stopped before something.

A voice in the dark intoned: "Kneel before His High Most Excellent, Illustrious, Glorious, and Most Rotund Lordship, Lord of the Great Burrows of Underhill and Barrowmere, High King Under the Earth—King Uhm."

Viola and Pall knelt on the cold stone. Tim knelt on Viola's shoulder, which is no small feat when one's legs don't have knees.

There was a long silence, broken only by the sound of chewing. Then swallowing. Then more chewing.

At last, cutlery clicked against a plate. Scuffling followed. Then came a tremendous scraping noise, accompanied by grunts—like several large mole-men straining to push something extremely heavy. Which, as it happened, they were: the very rotund King Uhm, seated upon his very large stone throne.

The scraping stopped directly in front of them.

A cough.

A bit more shuffling for final adjustments.

Then the King spoke.

Chapter 21

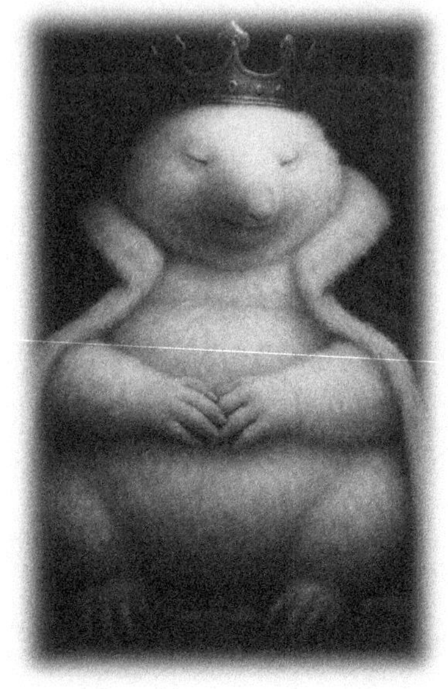

The darkness before them wasn't simply dark. It was the sort of dark that had opinions about itself. It loomed. It pressed. It suggested, quite firmly, that seeing things was overrated.

Viola could make out nothing of the King except an enormous mass of deeper shadow. The air itself seemed to bend around him, as though his presence had weight. Which, given what she'd heard about King Uhm, it probably did.

Then he spoke.

"Well," came a voice like a squeaky door hinge trapped inside a very large teapot, "you're shorter than I expected."

Viola blinked in the darkness. The King's voice was high, nasal, and oddly delicate. It sounded like a voice that belonged in a chipmunk or a mouse. But it had just emerged from what felt like a mountain.

"Your Majesty," she said, bowing her head. "Thank you for granting us audience."

"Mmm," squeaked the King. Stone groaned as he adjusted himself on his throne. "I don't usually grant audiences to surface-dwellers. Smelly creatures. All that fresh air." He sniffed. "But I was told you came with something interesting."

"We did, Your Majesty," Viola said. "A request, if it pleases you."

"Requests rarely please me. But do go on."

"We seek the location of the Queen of the Brean locusts. We were told—by the Queen of the wood-elves—that you know all things beneath the earth."

There was a long pause. Then a sound that might have been a chuckle, though it came out like a deflating balloon. Hee hee!

Around them in the dark, other Talpan laughed along. If the King laughed, the court laughed. That was, in fact, the law.

"The wood-elf queen told you that, did she?" The King's voice softened, wistful. "Ah. Such wisdom. Such grace. You can hear it in the way she moves the air. Did she… mention me, by chance?"

Viola hesitated. "She said you were very knowledgeable, Your Majesty."

"Knowledgeable!" The King sighed, a long whistle. "Yes. I suppose that's something. Though I had hoped…" He rallied. "Well. She met me once, you know. Just once. But I could tell she was quite taken with me. Who wouldn't be? I am, after all, the most eminent of all Talpan kings. The most rotund. My girth flows over the throne."

"Well, darkness has one benefit," Pall said. "Certain sights we don't need to see."

"Bite your tongue!" the King shouted. "Sight is for ignorant races. Talpan *feel* the glory." The way he said feel made clear he was rubbing his clawed hands over himself, pleased with his largeness.

Pall shuddered at the thought.

"In any event," the King continued, "I've been waiting for the right moment to send her a token of my affection. Something to remind her that I am here. Waiting. Under the earth. As kings do."

Viola wondered if King Uhm was aware that Queen Isiiala was in a permanent relationship, but she said nothing.

"So. Here is what I propose. I will tell you where to find your locust queen. And in return, when you return to the forest—you will deliver a small gift to her from me."

Unhappy murmurs stirred the court. His lords did not approve of his taste in queens.

"Silence!" shrieked the King. His already high voice rose like a slide whistle and ended in a piercing squeal that made Viola cover her ears. The murmuring stopped.

"We're not going that way," Viola said.

"Not going that way?" The wistfulness vanished. "Then why should I help you at all?"

"I—well, that is—" Viola scrambled. "What I meant to say, Your Majesty, is that we hadn't planned to go that way. But plans can change. Hypothetically."

"Hypothetically," the King repeated, flat.

"Yes. For instance, if you were to help us, then perhaps—hypothetically—we could help you in return."

A considering silence.

"Hm. Acceptable. Barely."

Viola exhaled. Tim, perched on her shoulder, let out a faint, relieved buzz.

"Now then," said the King. "You say you want to find the locust queen. Foolish girl. You don't want to go where she is."

"Respectfully, Your Majesty," Viola said, "I rather need to."

"Need to! What could possibly be worth going into that nest of—" He paused, apparently remembering Tim. "That is, that nest of perfectly respectable but extraordinarily numerous insects."

"They've eaten our food," Viola said quietly. "And all the pricklepepper. The Dampenians are suffering. I'm not asking much. I just need to talk to the Queen."

Pall spoke up. "Your Majesty, if I may—we've heard the Talpan have had difficulties with the Brean as well. That some of your children might be going hungry."

A sharp intake of breath rippled through the court. Humhum and Numni, kneeling behind them, went very still.

"Who told you that?" the King demanded.

"Our guards… may have… mentioned it?" Pall said, tentative.

A sigh. Another whistling note. "Well. I suppose it's no secret. Yes, the locusts are troublesome. They eat our mushroom crops. They chatter endlessly about exercise, which distracts our diggers. And they are forever jogging through tunnels they have no permission to use." He shifted. "But we are managing. We Talpan always manage."

"Of course, Your Majesty," Viola said quickly. "But perhaps, if we could speak to the Queen, we might help both our peoples."

The King was quiet for a long moment.

"Very well," he said at last. "I will tell you. Though I think you're mad to go."

He cleared his throat, a rusty-gate squeak. "You'll need to go directly south through the Underhill burrow—which is mine, by the way—and then into the Barrowmere burrow—also mine. At the south end of Barrowmere there's a small underground stream. On the far side you'll find the problem."

"The problem?" Viola asked.

"The locusts," the King said. "And their guards. Whether the Queen will speak to you, I can't promise. But that's where she is."

"Thank you, Your Majesty," Viola said, relief flooding through her.

"Don't thank me," the King said. "You can't get in."

"What's that?"

"You're far too big."

"I'm sorry?"

"Too big," he repeated. "The Queen's palace is underground, yes, but it's built for insects. Very small passageways. Not at all like my glorious tunnels and halls. You'll never fit."

Viola's heart sank. "Oh."

"Yes. 'Oh' indeed! Hee hee!" He wheezed, and the court laughed with him, as required by law. "How did you think you'd get in? Persuade the worm-folk to shrink you? Hee hee hee!"

Pall's body stiffened. "Wait. That's possible?"

Silence.

"What?" said the King.

"Worm-folk shrinking," Pall said. "Is that actually possible?"

"Well… yes," the King admitted. "Technically. There are worm-wizards who have that sort of magic. But it's entirely impossible for you to persuade them. They're not nice like I am."

"Where are they?" Viola asked.

A sigh. "The worm-wizards live beneath the Zolodrev tree. But it's impossible to get there. The Zolodrev grows behind the walls of Molgorosk. Dreadful place. Guards and dogs everywhere, and everything is square." He shuddered, a sound like an enormous bowl of jiggling jelly. "As everyone knows, circles and round shapes are far superior to anything square."

This pronouncement was much more appreciated by the court. There were calls of "Hear, hear!" and "Quite so, Your Majesty!"

"How do we get there?" Pall pressed.

"You'd have to go up into Molgorodian territory," the King said. "Which means dealing with them and their awful architecture."

In the dark, Viola found Pall's hand.

"We'll manage," she said.

"We'll see," the King snorted. Then, after a pause: "Humhum. Numni. Step forward."

Shuffling as the two Burrow Guards moved closer.

"Yes, Your Majesty?" said Humhum.

"You will escort these surface-dwellers to the southern border. The Barrowmere exit. With haste."

"Yes, Your Majesty," they said together.

"Do this task well and I may consider you for junior King's Guard."

A whisper rose in the darkness. "Sire, you just gave Duurgr that post."

"Indeed?" The King paused. "Well then. Perhaps *upper* junior King's Guard. Or even *lower-middle* might be in the offing."

A collective gasp. Somewhere, Duurgr ground his teeth.

Numni's voice, suddenly enthusiastic: "We'll have them out with utmost efficiency, Your Majesty."

"See that you do." Then, more quietly: "And girl. Surface girl."

"Yes, Your Majesty?" Viola said.

"Come here."

Viola stood and stepped forward carefully. Her hand met the King's belly. It was slightly furry and extremely soft.

"Oh! I'm sorry!" She pulled her hand back.

"What? For what?"

"For… touching you?"

"Of course! Touching is the only way." His squeaky voice came closer. "You are fortunate. Many of my court have never been granted the privilege of touching my majesty. Now, place your hand again, where I can feel it."

She did as told and pressed his yielding belly. A large paw found her hand and pressed into it something round and smooth, like an egg.

"Thank you," she said, slipping it into her pocket.

"Don't forget our arrangement. When you pass by the wood-elf queen's territory—and you will pass by it, hypothetically or otherwise—you will take my token to her."

"Of course, Your Majesty."

"Good." He settled back with a satisfied sound. "Dismissed."

The huffing and scraping began again—the throne being pushed away. The King's enormous shadow retreated into the larger dark.

Humhum touched Viola's hand. "Come along," he said. "We have rhinos to catch."

"Rhinos," Pall muttered as they stood. "Why don't I like the sound of that?"

"Because you're clever," Numni said briskly. "Now hurry up. I have a promotion to earn."

Chapter 22

hey followed guardmoles Humhum and Numni out of the King's chamber and down through twisting dark tunnels. The air turned earthy again and the walls pressed close.

As they descended, a peculiar sound began—a distant, washing rumble that seemed to come from the bones of the earth. It grew steadily louder.

"What's that?" came Pall's worried voice in the dark.

"The Speedway," said Numni with pride.

"The what?" said Viola.

"The King's road," added Humhum. "It connects the burrows. Very fast. Very safe. Mostly." He coughed. "Statistically."

Humhum pushed open a stone door, and the muffled growl burst out and became a roar—a thunder of pounding feet, scraping soil, and deep, eager chittering. Wind pressed against their faces, warm and gritty, carrying the smell of freshly turned clay.

They stepped into a vast chamber carved clean from the earth. The tunnel ahead was perfectly round—ten moles high at least. To one side it ended at a clay wall; to the other it ran off into darkness. Lines of yellowish crystals dashed along floor, wall, and ceiling, glowing faintly—just enough to reveal the scale of the cavern and the shapes moving within it.

Then the thunder showed its feet.

A rhinoceros beetle the size of a cart came charging past, armour plates gleaming, horn curved like a kettle handle. On its back rode a Talpan courier. The beetle's six legs worked in fierce delight. It loved running; anyone could see that. It loved it the way rivers love downhill.

At the far end it slowed, let off its rider with a few courteous clicks, and trotted back into the dark.

Viola leaned over the rail and had to shout to be heard. "HOW DO YOU KEEP THEM FROM CRASHING?"

"RULES!" called Numni, as though that explained everything.

Pall made the sort of face one makes when a baker cheerfully says, "Just add a pinch of dragon."

"WHAT RULES?!" Viola shouted.

"IT'S VERY SIMPLE!" bellowed Humhum, pointing into the blur of motion. "NORTHBOUND KEEPS RIGHT OF THE FLOOR LINES. SOUTHBOUND KEEPS LEFT. CEILING IS FOR

OVERTAKES—UNLESS IT'S A CEILING WEEK, THEN USE THE FLOOR. FAST RUNNERS USE THE LANE ONE OVER. IF THERE'S A BUM BUMPER, PULL TWO OVER. EVERY OTHER WEEK SWITCH ONE LINE TO THE RIGHT—UNLESS THERE'S CONSTRUCTION!"

"WHICH THERE ALMOST ALWAYS IS!" added Numni.

Viola tried to follow without success. "AND EVERYONE UNDERSTANDS?"

"OF COURSE!" said Numni.

Pall turned a careful shade of despair.

They descended to the mounting station—a tidy platform cut into the tunnel wall, striped posts at its edge, and a sign in firm dots and scratches: PLEASE ARGUE OFF THE TRACK. Beetles queued neatly for fares. Others, on break, clung to the walls and ceiling in easy conversation.

A clerk sat in a booth, nose twitching. "WHAT IS THAT AWFUL SMELL?"

"HUMANS!" shouted Numni. "AND A LOCUST! KING'S ORDERS!"

The clerk covered his nose and waved them through.

Arrangements were made: Pall and Numni would take the first beetle; Viola and Humhum the second.

Unfortunately, just as they were about to mount, the lead beetle and Tim got into words—very unpleasant ones.

Now, some time ago I explained that locusts don't speak Common. That is not entirely correct. They don't speak *human* Common. But they do speak *insect* Common. So do rhinoceros beetles—being insects themselves. And if, for example, you were a beetle with poor opinions about locusts (perhaps because some had been known to ride the Speedway without paying their fare), you might—hypothetically—say something rude in that language.

And in this case, you would be quite right to imagine so.

A lull came between passing beetles. Into that lull, the first beetle clicked something followed by a sound that, in insect Common, was extremely impolite.

Tim heard it.

Despite being roughly a thousand times smaller than his opponent, he hopped straight down and began chittering furiously. The exchange that followed was not suitable for children's ears. Humhum and Numni, who knew a few words of Insect, looked scandalized.

"Language!" declared Numni.

The clerk intervened, reprimanding the beetle for bad manners and telling it to leave the line. It clicked angrily, refusing to accept that forming opinions about someone's species was rude, uncalled for, and usually wrong. But in the end it stormed off, and the clerk offered his apologies.

Order, at last, re-established itself—rather shakily, but with dignity. Numni and Pall—Tim included—were seated on a new ride. Tim received proper courtesy, which helped, though he still looked miffed.

In all the excitement, Pall forgot to be afraid until the very last moment. By then it was too late. A horn sounded, and the beetle charged down the tunnel, Pall's scream following faithfully behind.

The next beetle pulled up. Humhum mounted with a polite *click-click* of the tongue—a greeting, apparently, for the beetle answered in kind.

Viola took a deep breath and climbed carefully onto the beetle's broad back, the shell warm and alive beneath her palms. Its plates shifted once, as if drawing breath. There seemed to be nowhere sensible to hold, so she held on to Humhum.

The horn sounded, and the world became wind.

The beetle lunged forward. Viola's stomach stayed briefly behind, then caught up with an apology. Her eyes streamed. She tasted speed. Her teeth clicked with every stride, but she

couldn't stop grinning. It felt like flying without permission—the ground drumming along to keep up.

The beetle twisted through the Speedway faster and faster. The glowing lines blurred, then fused into a single ribbon of light.

At last, the south exit appeared, flanked by two sleepy guards and a sign that read: PLEASE ENTER CALMLY. The tunnel narrowed; a gust of wet air struck Viola's face, and they burst into the southern burrow.

They slowed in long, rubbery strides, coasting to the platform.

Viola slid off and discovered her legs still believed in motion.

Pall lay on the ground, attempting to put himself back together. "Next time," he said weakly, "perhaps we can find a slow beetle. Or a slug."

"Those *are* the slow beetles," said Numni. "You should see the fire beetles."

Pall blanched. "I'd rather not."

The drivers settled, steam puffing softly from under their armour.

Before Tim's beetle took another fare, it clicked a few quiet notes toward him—clearly an apology. Tim looked startled, then answered with a short *bzz-bzz*, lifted his hat, and bowed. The beetle dipped its horn in return and trotted off into the dark.

And there you have it. One really should judge anyone only by their own actions—be they locust or beetle.

After a final climb upward and a winding walk through the tunnels of Barrowmere Burrow, our heroes reached the south gate. Humhum and Numni greeted their fellow guards. There was the usual discussion about the horrors of light and open air, but in the end the gate was opened—a cautious hand's width, then wider when no catastrophe occurred.

"Good," said Viola.

Pall blinked at the doorway. Daylight, thin as milk, spilled down the last slope of tunnel. After so long underground, real light was shocking.

They stepped forward together. The moles paused at the threshold, content with their dark. Viola and Pall shouldered their packs and went on into the grey, where the air smelled of grass and damp clay and just a little dust—and where, for the moment, everything seemed willing to be seen.

one was the wild land of the north. Before them the country looked as if a giant had pressed it with a stamp and then checked his work with a ruler. Each farm was exactly square. In the same corner of every parcel sat a tidy little cube of a farmhouse, painted the identical shade of yellow. A short distance away—precisely the same distance—stood a larger red barn, every one so similar that if you turned your head and then looked back again you suspected someone had moved the same buildings around while you weren't looking.

The sky wasn't cloudy like a Dampenian sky, but there was a smattering of rain now and again, and the merfolk umbrellas came in handy, even if their colours were too loud for Pall. Even the rain seemed organized. It fell straight down in even lines, as if it had received a memo reading, "The shortest distance from cloud to ground is straight. Proceed thusly."

"Molgorod," Pall said, in the tone one might use with a splitting headache.

Viola pushed hair out of her eyes and took a deep breath. "It doesn't look dangerous," she said. "Just organized."

Pall shuddered. "That's more than organized. That's finished."

Tim peeped from the hole in Pall's pocket, gave a nervous trill, and ducked back out of sight.

"Well," Viola said, "at least the road is nice."

It ran south in a perfect arrow, paved with flat stones fitted so closely that nothing grew between them. Not a speck of dirt marred it.

Before long, the question of how it remained so clean was answered. A woman appeared ahead, sweeping the stones carefully, block by block. She wore a plain dress, had cloth bags over her shoes, tied neatly at the ankles, and a somewhat rectangular head.

Viola brightened. "Good afternoon," she called.

The woman paused. She regarded them, then regarded the section of road where they had just been. She did not seem to approve.

"We are going to Molgorosk," Viola added cheerfully. "Can you give us directions?"

"Obviously not. Directions are not bricks."

"Pardon?"

"I can't give you pardon either," said the woman, frowning.

Now, I should explain something. Molgorodians like order and rules and everything just so. When they speak, they are precise. So precise that one must be very careful about how one speaks to them, or else misunderstandings occur—such as the one that had just happened. Viola should have said, *Will you please tell us the way to Molgorosk?* But not being familiar with how literal Molgorodians are in their thinking, she did not.

The woman looked at their umbrellas. "Where did you come from, and why are you so strange?"

"We're from Dampenia," said Pall.

"Never heard of it."

"It's a lovely country," Viola put in, "especially if you like the rain."

"I don't like the rain. Rain causes mud. Such as the mud you are tracking on the road."

Viola looked behind and discovered they were. The road had been perfect and now contained two faint paths of footprints.

"I'm sorry," she said.

"I didn't ask for your name, but at least that information is of use. Miss Sorry, if you intend to reach Molgorosk you are walking on the wrong road."

Pall was about to say, "That's not her name," but Viola waved her hand to say it was fine. "Where is the *right* road?"

The woman pointed with her broom. "Proceed south to the next intersection. Turn east. Travel fifteen grid roads east to Czar's North Quadrant Road. Turn south. Then it is twenty-five grid roads to the capital."

Viola peered south. "I can't even see the next intersection."

"It exists," said the woman. "Visibility is not a requirement for existence."

"How far is one grid road?" Pall asked.

"One kilometre, of course."

Pall didn't know what a kilometre was. "How long will that take to walk to the capital?"

"How fast do you walk?"

"I don't know."

"Then neither do I."

The rain continued to fall in neat lines as if setting a good example.

Pall sighed. "Maybe we can demonstrate."

They walked round and round while the sweeper measured their pace. After a minute she nodded. "At your established speed, if sustained with no variance, your journey should take one thousand four hundred and nineteen molgrotes."

Viola blinked. "How long is that?"

"I just told you. One thousand four hundred and nineteen."

"How many molgrotes before nightfall?" Viola asked, coaxing the number into friendliness.

"One thousand."

Pall did the math. "So—a day and a half?"

"No. One day and four hundred and nineteen molgrotes," the woman corrected. "Assuming you do not stop to eat, sleep, or relieve yourselves. Therefore, likely longer."

Viola's grin wobbled. "We'll walk until we're tired and rest at the side of the road. At least we can't get lost."

"You can't lounge on the side of the road," the woman said, shocked. "You will receive a ticket for vagrancy."

"But we must sleep sometime!"

"Naturally. Purchase a room at a licensed rest house."

"But we don't have any money."

"Then you will need to earn it, or ask for shelter without payment."

"We don't know anyone," Viola said.

"That is false," said the woman. "You clearly know each other. You have the same umbrellas."

"I mean in Molgorod," Viola clarified.

"What wild claims! You clearly know me, and I am in Molgorod."

Viola brightened. "Oh! Would you house us tonight?"

The woman stared. "If you can turn into a house, why do you need me? Besides, you stated that you seek Molgorosk. If you house yourself, you will not move."

Pall began to understand their problem. He chose his next words carefully. "Based on our walking speed, and assuming we'll need to rest at night, is there somewhere we can rest without paying coin?"

The woman's posture softened by one measurable degree. "Why did you not say so? At your pace you will likely cover a sufficient distance before nightfall to reach my cousin's farm. There is a farm in the southeast quadrant at First West and Fourteen North. My cousin Johnson operates it."

"Johnson," Viola repeated, liking the sound of the name.

"He is a strange man, but I am confident if you ask politely," the woman went on, "and say that I sent you, he will give you food and shelter."

"How do we get there?" Pall asked.

"Simple." She pointed. "Keep south to road Fourteen North. When you get there, turn east. Then proceed on Fourteen North to First West. There, in the southwest quadrant, you will find Johnson's farm."

"Who should I say has sent us?" Viola asked, politely, as the sweeping woman had not given them her name.

The old woman tilted her head. "Who should you say? Why me, of course. Saradaughter."

"Thank you," Viola said.

"For what?"

"For giving us directions," Viola said, then added, "even though they aren't bricks."

They moved on, and the woman began vigorously scrubbing the mud off the road behind them, shaking her head at their strangeness.

Eventually, the intersection came into view. Their north–south road was crossed by one running exactly east–west. A square signpost, shaped sort of like a mailbox—if a mailbox had no slot and just a flat top—stood where the roads met. One side of the signpost read, 28 N. The next side over read, 15 W.

"If we're at twenty-eighth, and we need fourteenth, then it's fourteen grids south," Pall concluded.

They walked south on 15 W and the numbers on the cubic signposts began counting down: 27 N, then 26 N, 25 N, and so on. The road never bent.

"Do you think all their houses are cubes because they like to be the same," Viola asked after a while, "or because someone told them that's what they had to be?"

"I'm not sure Molgorodians like anything at all," Pall said.

By 20 N the neat fields were beginning to blur together. Except for the signposts, it felt like they weren't making progress at all, because everything was exactly the same. They passed a field, reached a yellow cube with its red barn, then after a long walk saw what looked exactly like the same pair again.

"If we're lost, how would we even know?" Viola asked.

"We probably are already," Pall said.

Tim had not reappeared. When Pall checked, the little locust was curled in the pocket, trembling. The open geometry and perfect order frightened him more than any darkness had.

He had reason. The Czar's *Order 999*—to end the Brean "problem" permanently—had come from this land. Here, he was vermin. If discovered, there would be no mercy.

"Oh, Tim!" Viola said softly. "We'll keep you safe."

And though Tim was grateful, he likely thought, *What can a locust and two children do?* Most people think the world too dangerous to fix. But most people are not Viola, and her sort of hope was quite powerful, as we shall see.

At last, they reached 14 N and turned east.

Slowly the numbers ticked down: 14 W, 13 W, and so on. The rain fell straight, as if it might get a ticket if it dropped any other way.

By 6 W their legs ached. By 3 W, the sun was beginning to slide down the sky.

The southeast corner of 14 N × 1 W held a farm placed perfectly square upon the earth, as if printed there and allowed to dry.

Johnson's gate had hinges that neither squeaked nor dared. The path to the house ran in a ruler-straight line between rows of the officially approved green shrub for paths to houses. A square bell hung by the door, its rope cut to the exact length needed to pull.

"Shall I?" Viola asked.

"Yes," Pall said. "But only once. More may be illegal."

She rang exactly once.

A Molgorodian man appeared, square head tilted slightly down to regard them. He did not greet them; greetings serve no purpose. He waited patiently for what they would say.

"We are travellers," Viola said steadily. "Trying to reach Molgorosk. We've walked all day and are tired. We need a place to sleep, and Saradaughter, whom we met on the road, said you might let us stay."

"We're willing to work," added Pall.

The man blinked, then nodded. "Come. Remove your shoes at the door. You will eat, then bed. In the morning, you will work."

They placed their shoes beside the door, tidily, and stepped inside.

It was a perfectly lovely home, by Molgorodian standards: everything useful, nothing wasted. A kitchen with a cubic table and matching chairs. A straight staircase whose steps were precisely identical. A sitting room with a rectangular couch and a small geometric table before it, bearing a half-finished wooden puzzle. No art. No decoration. Only a square lantern for light and a rectangular stove for heat.

And there was a Doberman—perfectly black, perfectly still. Its eyes followed them. Its nose twitched once. Pall covered his pocket to mask Tim's scent.

"This way," said Johnson, leading them upstairs. On the second floor was a bedroom. It looked like it had never been used. "Place your things here," he said, then turned and went down the stairs.

They closed the door, coaxed Tim from Pall's pocket, and placed him on the bed. The poor locust trembled so badly his tiny sweater shook.

"Stay here," Viola said. "We'll bring food up."

"And don't speak," Pall warned. "Dogs can hear Locust."

Tim nodded weakly.

Downstairs, Johnson had laid out dried fruit, dried meat, dried bread, and water. They thanked him, which confused him.

"You have agreed to work, and I have agreed to lodging," he said, though not unkindly.

"We do appreciate your kindness, nonetheless," she answered.

There was nothing to say to that, so he just stared at them eating.

"Are you going to eat?" Viola asked.

"I have eaten."

It felt uncomfortable just being watched while eating, so Viola attempted to make conversation. "You have a lovely home," she said.

"It meets all the requirements," Johnson responded with a nod. But he offered no talk in return. He just watched them eat.

She tried again. "Did you build it yourself?"

"No."

After another pause, Pall offered, "You don't talk much, do you?"

Johnson seemed confused. "I speak when information is needed."

"Sometimes," Pall explained, "it is good to talk without a purpose."

"That is odd," he answered.

But he did think of something to say. Foreigners are rare in Molgorod, owing to all the rules and the lack of small talk, so he asked, "Where have you come from?"

"Dampenia," said Viola. "A small kingdom to the west."

Having had that success, he tried another. "Where are your parents?"

To her surprise, Viola felt very homesick and began to cry. "I'm sorry," she said. "I'm just tired, I think."

Now, you might think Molgorodians like Johnson are heartless. They are not. They are practical. Yet they cry, too—usually when a tower collapses after twenty years of perfect planning.

Still, Johnson was distressed to see Viola cry. "Have you lost your parents? Perhaps we can find them."

Viola said that was kind but no. Then she explained everything: the boggarts, the merfolk, the locusts;

how she thought something should be done and so she did, and how one thing had led to another until she was here, trying to get to the Zolodrev tree in Molgorosk, hoping to be shrunk so she might ask the Queen of the Brean not to eat all the pricklepepper. The longer she talked, the more hopeless it felt, until she ran out of words and simply sat in the rectangular chair, crying quietly.

Johnson listened without interrupting. Though he found her strange, he admired her persistence. Practical people respect persistence. He had never had a child, but he had always wanted one. And despite her strangeness, his heart went out to her, and he resolved that if there was something he could do to help, he would.

Chapter 24

"Worms are wonderful creatures. So useful. They turn waste into soil. Soil into food. Very efficient."

Johnson stood at the sink, washing the rectangular plates with rectangular motions.

"I have never heard of worm-wizards beneath Molgorosk," he said, placing a plate at an exact angle on the drying rack. "But if such creatures exist, they would likely be beneath the Zolodrev."

Viola sat up straighter. "Do you know where it is?"

"Yes, of course. It grows in the Royal Botanical Gardens of the Czar."

"Oh no," Viola said, her voice shrinking. "Will we need to see the Czar? We really aren't special."

Pall immediately disagreed. "You've spoken to the queen of the wood-elves and the King of the Talpan. And you're the only one in all Dampenia doing something about the locusts. I think you're special."

"The royal gardens are a national treasure," Johnson answered. "They are open to everyone. The Czar is generous in this regard. Besides, horticulture is educational. And nutritious."

He dried his hands on a towel and folded it into a perfect square.

"I will help you. The capital is a short journey south. Tomorrow we will take Horse and go together."

Viola blinked. "You'd help?"

"Yes. I need to. You do not know the way."

"But what about your farm?" Viola asked.

"I will ask my neighbours to water and weed. Dog will guard."

"That is very kind of you."

Johnson paused, considering. "I want to help."

He looked at them both with something that was not quite a smile, but near enough.

"Have you finished your food?"

Viola had planned to slip some food into her pocket, but it felt wrong to sneak when Johnson was so kind. She took a breath.

"Johnson, may I take the rest of my food to my room?"

Johnson tilted his head slightly. "This is the eating room. The purpose of the bedroom is sleep, not eating."

"Still," Viola said carefully, "I'd like to take some food up with me."

"It seems very unusual. And impractical." He adjusted the towel, though it had seemed perfectly straight already. "If you take food upstairs, then you will need to take the plate upstairs. An unnecessary bit of carrying. Also, there could be crumbs in the bedroom, which will require extra cleaning. And the cleaning supplies are down here."

Pall cleared his throat. "Eating in a bedroom is common in Dampenia. It's our custom."

Johnson frowned. "I see."

"I won't take a plate," Viola added quickly. "I'll carry the food in my hand. And I promise not to make a mess."

Johnson considered. "Very well. It seems like a strange custom, but I will allow it."

Viola gathered the fruit and started up the stairs. Pall followed.

Tim had not moved from the spot where they had left him. He sat on the bed, a tiny piece of the bed sheet wrapped around him like a cloak, his large eyes fixed on the door.

He perked up when Viola produced the leftover dried fruit.

"Here," she whispered. "Eat."

Tim chirped softly and reached for the fruit with trembling legs.

Pall pointed out quietly that, given the way Tim ate, there was likely about to be an explosion of fruit. And they had promised no mess.

Viola paused. Then she opened the nearest dresser drawer. It was empty. She set Tim inside, put in the fruit, and closed it.

A moment later they heard a muffled sound like a saw racing through wood.

When she opened the drawer again, the inside was speckled with fruit and tiny seeds, but she wiped it clean. Tim, now full and drowsy, decided he felt safer from the dog in the drawer. The wooden walls muffled sound. The darkness was comforting.

So he stayed.

Pall took the other narrow cot by the window, which overlooked the perfectly square fields stretching

into the dusk. Soon he was asleep.

Viola lay awake a long time, thinking about all the strange things in the world and wondering if her mother missed her as much as she missed home. She wished there were a way to send a message—a bird, perhaps, or a very organized mail system. Molgorod likely had one, though she doubted it would deliver to Dampenia without the proper paperwork. She worried about whether she'd ever find the Queen of the Brean. She worried about whether she'd be able to find her way home. She worried about the last pricklepepper sitting on the table back in Dropminster, and whether it had been found and eaten. She worried about Tim, hidden in a drawer, trembling because the world wanted him gone. Eventually she fell asleep and had worried dreams about forgetting her keys and being unable to remember where she had put them.

Chapter 25

They woke to sunshine.

It took some getting used to—not waking to grey and rain. The land outside their window was bright and cheerful, even if perfectly organized.

Viola told herself, *I set myself on this path, and I need to finish it, whatever it takes.* A very practical thought. Johnson would have approved.

He was already outside when they joined him. Dog sat perfectly still beside him.

"Good morning!" Viola called.

He looked puzzled for a moment, then nodded. "Talking without purpose." He turned back to his farm. "It rained yesterday, and the sun is up, so the crops are growing. That makes it good. And it is morning."

Viola smiled.

Pall said, "We're ready to work."

"That is also good," said Johnson. "And I have a very important job for you."

He led them to the barn. There, laid in perfect stacks, was a large pile of bricks.

"You see the problem," said Johnson.

They did not. The stacks looked flawless.

"They need to be used?" Pall guessed.

"No. But they might be, someday. Look—mismatched sides. Truly distressing."

It was true: one side of each brick was lighter from the sun, the other darker. The solution, of course, was to restack them facing the opposite way.

So they did. All morning. Viola and Pall turned each brick and rebuilt the pile. Johnson trimmed the nearby grass until it matched exactly and then nodded, deeply satisfied. Dog sat one pace to his left the entire time, watching.

A neighbour leaned over the hedge. "You are turning the brick pile!"

"Yes," said Johnson. "With time, the sides will match again."

"That is a very good thing."

"I agree."

They admired the new stack. Clearly, a triumph.

After lunch they gathered their things. Johnson brought Horse and the cart around. Tim was hidden in Pall's pocket as they came out of the house. Johnson sat waiting on the cart. Dog sat beside it, watching.

Then came a faint buzz from Pall's coat. Tim had sneezed.

Dog's head snapped around. He sniffed once, growled, and launched.

Pall stumbled back. Tim shot out in panic and began hopping frantically. Dog darted after, jaws snapping—once, twice—teeth bared.

Without thinking, Viola threw herself in the way. Dog's teeth closed on her sleeve, tearing cloth and stopping inches from Tim.

"Stop! He's mine!" she shouted.

"Dog. Sit," said Johnson.

Dog froze mid-lunge and sat, calm as stone.

Johnson took Viola's hand and examined her wound. "It is not serious," he said after a moment. Then he looked from her torn sleeve to the trembling locust. "Why," he asked, "do you have a Brean?"

"This is Tim. He's my friend," said Viola. "He hasn't hurt anyone."

Pall spoke quickly. "We need him to speak to the Queen of the Brean."

A pause. Dog waited for the order to kill.

Then Johnson said, "If you intend to persuade the Queen of the Brean locusts, it is logical that you need a Brean to speak for you."

They exhaled.

"However, *Order 999* remains the law. Tim should not have come to Molgorod. Every family has a dog, and every dog will be able to hear and smell him. When he is discovered, he will be destroyed."

Viola looked up at Johnson. "Please. I can't abandon him. Pall's right. We need him."

Tim hid behind Viola's torn sleeve, waiting for the end.

Johnson considered Tim in silence. Then, after careful thought, he went into the house. A minute later he returned with a glass jar pierced for air and a bag of garlic cloves. "If you cannot abandon your locust, you must hide him. This jar will capture sound. Garlic has a very strong odour. I cannot guarantee that this plan will work, but if Tim hides in this jar, surrounded by garlic cloves, he may avoid being found."

Tim crawled in and began eating garlic for courage. Fortunately, Johnson had a great deal of garlic.

Pall turned to Johnson. "Aren't you breaking the law?"

"Yes."

"Will you get in trouble?"

"If Tim is discovered, then that is likely."

"Why would you do that for us? We've just met."

"You will not succeed in your quest without my help," he answered calmly. "And I said that I would help. For me to keep my promise, I must take that risk."

Johnson's farm lay on the first road west; the next north–south road was Czar's North Quadrant Road—twice as wide, smooth enough to reflect the sky, with a bright red line down the centre. Johnson drove Horse on the right side. Other travellers moved around them in perfect order, silent. Greetings were not the Molgorodian way.

"Johnson," Viola asked, "why don't you use the room we stayed in?"

"It is a children's room," said Johnson. "It is to be slept in by children."

"Do you have children?"

"I do not."

"Do you have a wife?"

"I do not."

"Why not?"

He turned and looked at her. "I am not desired."

"But you are very kind! Surely there are lots of Molgorodian women who would like you."

He turned back to the road. "You value kindness. But that is not a quality that is highly valued in my country."

"Well—it is in Dampenia."

He thought about that for a while.

As they travelled south, lines appeared on the road. It became a very dull rainbow. They arrived at the city of Molgorosk. Its grey walls stood firm and solid under a pale sky, and behind them, towers stacked like bricks reached for the clouds. Travellers were lined up on the rainbow lines. At the front of each line, a guard with a dog checked travellers' paperwork.

At the gate, a long line of travellers waited before a booth with a sign that read: QUEUE HERE TO QUEUE.

Johnson joined the line.

"Why aren't we going in?" Pall asked.

"We need to know which line to stand in," Johnson answered.

Eventually they reached the front and spoke with the clerk.

"Destination?"

"The Royal Botanical Gardens."

"Blue line." He handed them a blue ticket.

Then they joined the blue line and queued again.

Viola watched the guard. He checked each visitor and their paperwork. The dog would walk around them, sniffing.

As they inched forward, she became more and more worried they'd find Tim. She glanced at Pall. He gripped his spear tightly, ready to use it. She took off her pack that held Tim's jar and hugged it.

Finally, it was their turn.

"Ticket," the guard said.

Johnson gave him the blue ticket. His dog approached Viola. Its black eyes stared into hers, as if measuring her fear. It sniffed her bag. Its nose wrinkled. It moved on. Finally, it went and sat by the guard again.

"Enter," said the guard. "Stay on blue."

Inside, the capital spread vast and orderly. There were so many people, and most of them had Dobermans walking exactly beside them. Everyone stayed on their line. They moved with purpose, no one greeted anyone, and no one smiled. Other than the sound of marching footsteps, it was almost silent. It felt less like a city and more like a giant machine.

They passed a man in a yellow hat measuring pedestrians' strides with a ruler. A whistle blew. Someone got a ticket because their left step was longer than their right.

A light rain started falling, and that made her feel better. A little tune popped into Viola's head, so she hummed it. Too late, she realized everyone was staring. The tune stumbled and disappeared.

"Why were you making that noise?" Johnson asked. He looked at her as if she had suddenly sprouted wings.

"Sometimes I hear music in the rain, and I just hum along," Viola answered.

"Music," he said, unfamiliar with the word. "Does it do anything?"

"Um… makes me happy? I think that's about it." Then she whispered, "Am I in trouble?"

Johnson was thoughtful. Then he said, "I suppose there's no law against it, as no one has ever thought to do it."

At last, they reached a great stone arch that read: THE GRAND ROYAL BOTANICAL GARDENS OF CZAR VORTAN.

Inside, trees stood in ranked rows like soldiers. Citizens harvested fruit into numbered baskets. Dogs ate the fallen produce. Viola kept Tim hidden; the garlic fooled the noses.

They came upon a crowd of people. A sign read: NATIONAL SQUARE-APPLE FINALS.

Farmers proudly displayed cubed apples on stands. Several judges were examining the finalists.

Johnson turned to Viola with a smile. "Good day! The whole country competes, and only the very best reach the finals. The winner is a national hero, and you may witness it."

After a moment, Johnson's eyes lit up. "I have a talking without purpose," he said. "Do you wish to hear it?"

"Yes, very much," Viola answered.

"Apple number three is superior."

The farmer with apple number three stood a little taller.

Pall peered at the fruit. It looked exactly like all the others. "I can't see a difference."

"Can you not see the difference? This one looks so nutritionally dense!"

And Johnson was proved right. A few minutes later, one of the judges came and stood before farmer number three and gave him a golden trophy. Everyone clapped.

Johnson wiped away a tear.

"Johnson, are you crying?" Viola asked.

"So beautiful. A perfect apple. And I was here to see it." He breathed deeply, enjoying the moment.

The crowd started to leave.

Viola realized something. "Johnson?"

"Yes?"

"That beautiful feeling you have? That's how music feels."

"Fascinating," Johnson said. "But sound is not nutritious."

"I'm not sure," Viola answered. "Sometimes it feels like it is."

The Zolodrev stood at the garden's centre. It was ancient. Its bark was gnarled. From its branches hung hundreds of small cubed golden fruit. It was blocked off by a large square fence, and on each side there was a sign that read: DO NOT EAT. At each corner of the fence stood a guard,

and beside each guard a Doberman.

"This is the Zolodrev," Johnson said.

"I didn't know it was guarded and off-limits!" Viola exclaimed.

"It is one of the Czar's greatest treasures," Johnson explained. "The only plant in the world that naturally grows cubed fruit. Also, the Brean nearly took all the fruit, which led to the law requiring their execution."

"Wait," Pall replied. "I thought *Order 999* was because Molgorodian dogs went out of control?"

Johnson looked at him. "That is also true. However, it was when the Queen of the Brean ordered her armies to take the fruit that the Czar acted."

"Why did she try to take the fruit?"

"I do not know."

"Didn't anyone ask?"

Johnson was puzzled. "Why would the reason matter? It is wrong and punishment is required."

Pall was looking at the guards and dogs. "Well, we've made it. But now what?"

The soil under the Zolodrev was so dark it was almost black. A small worm wiggled near Viola's boot.

Viola crouched. "Hello," she said softly.

It didn't respond. It just wiggled back into the soil.

Pall found another.

She knelt again. "Hello? We're looking for the worm-wizards."

But though she tried repeatedly, the worms just ignored her.

Johnson folded his hands. "They do not appear to have ears. Perhaps they cannot hear you."

Viola sighed. "Maybe these aren't the right worms."

From inside her pack came a faint *tap-tap-tap* on glass.

Viola opened the flap. Tim pounded his tiny chest, then pointed downward and moved his arms like he was digging.

"But Tim, there are guards and dogs!" she whispered. "Are you sure?"

Tim nodded bravely.

The heroes slipped behind a nearby shrub. Viola lifted the jar and tipped it gently.

Tim adjusted his tiny hat and rolled up his sleeves. He looked both ways for Dobermans, then popped out of the jar and began to dig.

Chapter 26

Tim burrowed straight down, claws scrabbling, until the world above was only muffled rain. Underground, for a breath, he was safe.

Locusts, as you may recall, see perfectly well in the dark. They can also tell east from west even in solid earth. Tim went three feet down, then turned east toward the Zolodrev. The soil was loose—alive with worms—and he bumped into more than one, apologizing as he dug around them.

Now, worms have no eyes, or ears, or mouths, or any of the features most of us arrange upon our heads. What they *do* have is an extraordinary nose. They adore strong smells—the sort that make other creatures' eyes water—and take great pride in perfuming themselves. That is why they can so often be found wiggling through compost and other fragrant delights.

The soil beneath the great Zolodrev tree was their paradise: dark, rich, and faintly spicy. Yet it lacked one particular note—garlic. Tim, having spent far too long in Johnson's jar and eaten his fill of cloves, smelled precisely like it. He was irresistible. Before long, a number of hopeful young lady worms began following him, each convinced she had found a particularly dashing mate.

Tim dug faster. Not only did he think he was too young for marriage, but also he was the wrong species.

In his haste, he stopped paying attention to direction and suddenly burst through into a hollow space. He shot from the tunnel near the ceiling and fell almost a foot to the dirt floor below. A foot may not sound much to you, but when you are the size of a thumb it is quite a tumble. His boots flew one way, his hat another.

Something steadied him. Not a hand. A worm's head.

"Are you all right?" asked a soft voice.

"Leave him be!" said another.

Tim groaned. His eyes focused on the speaker—or rather, the speakers. Two heads upon one body, both wearing little silver rings around their necks.

"Let me help you," said the kind head.

"Oh, give it up," said the other. "You can't trust anyone who falls out of the ceiling."

You may have guessed it already: Tim had landed in the bedroom of a worm-wizard. A Zuzzuzian worm-wizard, to be precise. Centuries ago, most worms lost their thoughts in a magical accident known grimly as the Great Unworming, but a few families survived and continued to practise their art. They have no eyes but do possess noses, mouths, and fine manners. The finer sort also wear jewellery shaped as rings upon their bodies, which, if you think about it, is the most convenient place for a worm to wear jewellery.

The helpful head belonged to Zazila. The cross one was her twin, Zilili. Being young and rather vain, Zazila glittered with tiny bands of gold and silver. She was also, at that moment, completely smitten. The scent of garlic can do strange things to a worm.

Tim collected his boots, accepted his hat from her mouth, and bowed. "Thank you kindly."

Zazila blinked in delight. "Oh! You can speak!"

Worms, especially wizarding ones, are clever and multilingual; to her ears Tim sounded foreign but charming.

"Who is he," demanded Zilili, "and what does he want?"

"I am 93998544771114356," said Tim formally, "but you may call me Tim."

"Tim," repeated Zazila, sighing. Worm names generally include at least one Z. His did not, which only made it more exotic.

At that moment the tunnel wall bulged and two enormous heads appeared. Huzzan Zuzzat, the girls' father, was entering—or perhaps they were. Each half of him was large, fat, and very protective.

"I heard a crash," said Huzzan.

"And a smell," added Zuzzat suspiciously.

"Nothing, Daddy," said Zilili at once.

"This is Tim," said Zazila at the same time.

The fathers puffed up. "*Tim*? Who's Tim—and why is he in your bedroom?"

"Nothing happened!" said Zazila.

"It was all her doing!" said Zilili.

"Sirrah!" thundered Huzzan. "I ought to turn you into a grub!"

Tim's temper flickered. "If your grounds had proper paths—and maybe a few signs—I wouldn't have fallen through your ceiling!"

He bumped Huzzan right back.

The worms were astonished. Few creatures dared talk back to their father, who genuinely *could* turn someone into a grub, and occasionally did.

"Stop it!" cried Zilili.

"Please don't fight!" said Zazila. "I love him!"

Everyone froze. Then everyone spoke at once.

"You've only just met him!"

"There's been a misunderstanding!"

"Cheeky rogue!"

"Well," said Huzzan, thinking rapidly, "in that case, he must stay for dinner."

It turned out he had been trying for ages to marry off his daughters.

"Could one hope for noble birth?" asked Huzzan.

"One might hope," answered Zuzzat.

Taking Tim by both heads, they led him down the corridor, asking questions as they went.

"Where is your kingdom?"

"Are you a warrior?"

"How long have you been courting our daughters?"

Tim could hardly get a word in. At last, he stopped short. "Sirs, your daughters are charming, but I'm not here for them. I'm on a mission of national importance."

"A *quest* of importance," said Huzzan.

"A *person* of importance," said Zuzzat, deeply impressed.

They swept him into a wider chamber which was kitchen and dining room. Within, their mother, Marzia Brazia was cooking—and both of her heads looked as if they had seen far too many accidents already.

"Who is this?" asked Marzia.

"Everyone," said Huzzan, "this is Tim."

"He's a foreigner," added Zuzzat.

"He's mine," said Zazila.

"Zazila's in love again," sighed Zilili.

"Well then," said Brazia, "what have you to say for yourself?"

Tim removed his hat. "Ma'ams, there's been a misunderstanding. I'm not a worm."

Silence spread through the room like spilled ink.

Zuzzat turned purple. "A cross-species entanglement! Scandalous!"

Zazila burst into tears.

Huzzan coughed. "Well, love is blind."

Marzia comforted Zazila; Brazia scolded Zilili; everyone else looked uncertain what manners required next.

Tim then told them his story—how he had come from Dampenia, how his people had eaten all the pricklepepper, and how Viola was above even now, trying to make things right. The worms listened gravely. When he finished, they all shook their heads.

"The Brean," murmured one. "Such a pity."

"A terrible fate."

"And now," said another, "they go on eating forever."

Tim frowned. "What do you mean?"

Zilili looked at him sharply. "You truly don't know?"

He shook his head.

"How old are you?"

"Two years old."

"Then you've little more than one year left before the hunger takes you," she said.

He stared. "Before what?"

"The ravening," she said simply. "When a Brean grows beyond three years, the hunger consumes him. That is why your people are feared."

Tim's voice felt small. "And this will happen to me?"

"I'm afraid so. But once, it might have been prevented."

Huzzan spoke next. "Your queen searched for a cure. She found the Zolodrev tree. Its fruit can be chewed for hours, easing the hunger."

Marzia added, "She went to the Czar and begged him to share it."

"But he refused," said Brazia.

"And ordered your people destroyed!" cried Zazila, sobbing again.

Tim sank onto the floor. "Then even if Viola finds the Queen of the Brean, there's nothing she can do."

"I fear that's true," said Huzzan gently.

For a moment no one spoke. Then Tim drew himself up. "No. I won't accept it. If we must, I'll steal the fruit and bring it to my people."

Chapter 27

he worms whispered anxiously. Guards stood above with sharp teeth; even if he succeeded, he could carry only a few fruits.

"You would need a Zolodrev of your own," said Marzia.

"Then that," said Tim, "is what we'll have to grow."

"It's not that simple," said Zilili. "You'd need a Zolodrev seed, lots of water, and worm-magic."

Tim straightened. "Then I'll take a seed."

The twin fathers exchanged looks.

"You cannot simply pluck one," said Huzzan.

"They are guarded day and night by the Czar's finest," said Zuzzat.

"And their dogs," added Marzia.

"Vile creatures with noses instead of manners," muttered Brazia.

Tim thought of Viola and her torn sleeve. "There must be a way. I must save my people—and myself."

Zazila's rings jingled as she wiggled closer. "So brave," she sighed.

Zilili gave her a look. "So foolish," she said, though not without admiration. "But you have spirit, I'll give you that."

"I have friends above," said Tim suddenly. "They'll help. Viola will think of something."

At once Zazila froze. Despite being very sweet, she was prone to jealousy. "Who," she asked sweetly, "is Viola?"

"She's an extraordinary human," said Tim, without thinking. "She's the reason I'm here."

Zazila's glow dimmed. "Extraordinary," she repeated faintly, not at all liking the idea of Tim calling another female extraordinary.

"Indeed," said Zilili, smirking. "Perhaps you could tell us more about this extraordinary human."

Tim, unaware of Zazila's feelings, went on. "She's clever and brave. She speaks to kings and queens and never takes no for an answer. She's trying to reach the Queen of the Brean to save her people. And she's waiting for me in the garden."

The worms murmured among themselves.

"Waiting?" asked Huzzan. "Above ground?"

"Yes. With Pall—the hunchback boy—and Johnson, who's an unusually kind Molgorodian."

"A kind Molgorodian," said Zuzzat, deeply puzzled. "Are you sure?"

Tim nodded earnestly. "Viola needs your help. King Uhm said worm-magic could make her small enough to meet the Brean Queen. That's why she came to Molgorosk—not for the Zolodrev, but for you."

Huzzan blinked. "King Uhm, you say? The Talpan king?"

Tim nodded again.

"How under the earth did you get an audience with him?"

"It was Viola," said Tim simply. "She just doesn't stop until people listen."

The worms looked suitably impressed. Even Marzia's stern expression softened.

"Still," said Huzzan gravely, "you do not understand what you are asking. All magic is dangerous. But size-magic is very tricky. Sometimes it works. Sometimes it works too well. Sometimes you disappear entirely. And when it fades—if it fades—it can do so at the most inconvenient moment."

"Oh, Father," cried Zazila, recovering from her jealousy, "we must help him! He's so noble!"

Tim bowed. "Please, sir. What can I do to persuade you?"

The fathers withdrew to confer with Marzia Brazia, muttering in low tones.

Zazila immediately turned to Tim. "You mustn't worry. I shall convince them."

"I don't want to cause trouble," said Tim.

"You already have," said Zilili dryly. Then, softening, "But it's rather entertaining."

She tapped one of her rings. "You know, they still treat us like wormlets, even though we're nearly two years old."

The parents returned, arranged themselves solemnly, and declared, "We will discuss your future—over dinner."

Stone tables were dragged together. The air filled with the warm, swampy scent of worm cuisine. Marzia Brazia ordered the twins to set a place of honour for their guest.

Tim hesitated. "Viola's waiting," he said.

"Good manners first," said Brazia firmly. "Heroes may save the world on a full stomach."

So he stayed. Soon the table was heaped with the most pungent dishes imaginable: fermented-mulch soufflé, roasted-root slime, and something politely called *scent pudding*. Jugs of aged Zolodrev sap were brought out—a drink so spicy it would make your eyes water. Unless you were a Brean, in which case it would be the most wonderful drink you had ever tasted.

Tim worried about disgracing himself. However, as the food was largely smelly splots of mush, his appetite—once a menace—deserted him. He nibbled as politely as possible. The worms, mistaking restraint for refinement, were charmed.

"Such delicacy," whispered Marzia. "Remarkable for a Brean."

By the time the dishes were cleared, Tim had drunk several cups of sap—mostly by accident. The world swayed pleasantly. His hosts seemed friendlier by the minute. Zazila's laughter tinkled like jewellery. Zilili's remarks grew sharper and funnier.

Tim found himself telling stories. He described their journey through Slipwood, their escape from the Talpan, even the nose-ring in the well. The twins gasped and clasped their rings in awe. Worms cannot swim, so to them the tale was mythic.

When the table was cleared, Huzzan Zuzzat led Tim into the "men's parlour"—a smaller cave lined with jars of pickled air-roots.

"My boy," said Zuzzat, draping a neck round Tim's shoulders, "I wasn't sure about you at first, but you're all right."

"Thank you, sir," said Tim, trying to remain upright.

"Are you truly determined to save your people and help your friend?" asked Huzzan.

"Yes, sir. Whatever it takes."

The fathers exchanged approving nods.

"Well then," said Zuzzat, smiling broadly, "we have a proposal."

Tim blinked. "A proposal?"

"You are an eligible young locust," said Huzzan.

"And we have daughters about your age," said Zuzzat.

"They are very accomplished," added Huzzan. "Especially Zilili. Quite the enchantress."

"Zazila, of course, is… enthusiastic," said Zuzzat tactfully.

Tim, flushed with sap and flattery, nodded. "Yes, quite charming."

"Splendid," said Huzzan. "Then if you would propose—"

"And they were to accept—"

"We would be very much indebted to you," they finished together.

Tim blinked again. "Propose what, exactly?"

"Why, marriage, of course!" they chorused.

"A long engagement is just

the thing!" said Zuzzat.

Huzzan's head spun. He still smiled, but looked shocked. "A long engagement?! Not at all! We should get the wedding done tonight! No time like the present for love."

The two fathers fell to arguing. Though they had agreed on the idea of marrying off Zazila Zilili, being worms, they could not agree on the details.

Tim's jaw fell open. The walls seemed to tilt.

Chapter 28

"Propose," Tim repeated, his mind struggling to catch up with his tongue. The world still swayed pleasantly from the sap, but certain words had a way of sobering a locust. "As in marriage."

"As in embracing your future!" said Huzzan.

"Exactly so," said Zuzzat. "It would give us great happiness to offer our assistance to a young couple embarking upon a quest."

"Your assistance?" said Tim weakly.

"Naturally," said Huzzan. "Worm-magic, guidance through the roots, assistance for your friend Viola—anything a family might do for a son-in-law."

Zuzzat smiled in a way that contained, quite clearly, the idea of consequences. "Of course, should you decline, one could hardly blame my daughters for despair. And despair among young worm-wizards sometimes produces—accidents."

"Accidents," echoed Tim faintly.

His stomach did a small leap. He imagined being turned into a grub, which is the sort of thing that can happen if a wizard's patience runs short. He also imagined Zazila's cheerful rings and Zilili's elegant one, and the way both heads had bent toward him when he told his stories.

"This is unexpected," he said carefully. "Marriage is a large matter—larger even than quests." He took a breath, searching for a word that might mean yes and maybe simultaneously. "I would be honoured," he said at last. Perhaps it was all the sap he had drunk speaking, or perhaps it was the very real threat of being turned into a grub, or perhaps—and this surprised him most—he found he didn't entirely mind the idea.

"Excellent!" beamed Huzzan, and clapped him on the back.

"Most sensible," said Zuzzat, and gave him a friendly punch in the arm.

The fathers guided him back to the main chamber, where the mothers were baking something that smelled halfway between a rotten banana and an old tire.

"Well?" asked Brazia.

The fathers straightened importantly.

"Our dream will happen tonight!" said Huzzan.

"Great news—but no need to rush things," said Zuzzat.

The mothers exchanged looks.

"Oh," said Marzia. "How romantic."

Zazila looked up eagerly. "What's romantic?"

"Nothing yet," said Zilili. "But I suspect we're about to find out."

Marzia turned to Tim with a gracious smile. "The southern tunnels are lovely this time of evening. A short walk is just the thing."

"Oh, not the south!" objected Brazia. "The northern tunnels are much wider, and the soil smells sweeter."

They disagreed on which tunnels were finer, but they agreed that a romantic walk was exactly the thing. Marzia fetched Tim's hat; Brazia brushed it off and set it neatly on his head.

"Girls," she said, nudging Tim forward, "why don't you show Tim around."

The daughters followed—Zazila glowing, Zilili suspicious.

The door of earth closed softly behind them. Roots hung like thin curtains. The soil shifted from dry grit to damp velvet. Somewhere below, the ground ticked with worm-song. The air grew cooler, tasting of iron and fungus.

Zazila hummed, rings chiming against one another. "Isn't it a perfect evening? The soil smells like adventure."

Zilili sniffed. "It smells like fungus."

Tim trotted between them, boots scuffing the soft soil. He tried to focus on his breathing, his footing, and his probable doom. He had never proposed marriage. "Yes," he said. "Beautiful."

Zazila leaned nearer. "You're very quiet."

"He's thinking," said Zilili. "Or regretting."

Tim stopped walking. His stomach performed a slow revolution. "I am," he said, "attempting bravery."

"Ah!" said Zazila, delighted. "We'll wait."

"What if—" he began, and stalled.

Zazila swayed nearer. Rings chimed against rings.

He took a deep breath. He put one knee down. His hat fell over one eye in a way that was surely charming somewhere in the world. He lifted his face.

"Zazila. Zilili," he said solemnly, "would you do me the honour of being my wife?"

Zazila gasped so loudly the roots trembled. "Oh yes! Yes, yes, yes!"

Zilili tilted her head. "Are you out of your mind? We met this afternoon."

Tim remained kneeling, uncertain which answer was more dangerous. "Shall I—stand up now?"

Zilili sighed. "Please."

Zazila fluttered her rings. "You may."

He rose, brushing soil from his knees. "So—what does this mean?"

"No," said Zilili.

"Yes!" said Zazila.

They returned together to the chamber, where the families waited in hopeful silence.

"Well?" asked Huzzan.

"Madness!" said Zilili.

"Ecstasy!" said Zazila.

The parents considered.

"Halfway there," concluded Marzia. She nodded at Tim. "That's the right direction."

There was no sudden wedding ceremony, but everyone was satisfied that Tim had made a fine first step toward earning the love of their daughters. They toasted the young people's lives and hopes and dreams, and before long Tim started to think it wasn't such a bad idea after all to get married—if Zilili warmed to him, of course.

"We shall celebrate later," said Brazia. "For now, we must prepare for the surface."

"Yes," said Marzia. "The human girl needs help."

"The shrinking, you mean," said Huzzan. "Delicate work."

"Very delicate," said Zuzzat. "But safe enough if done with care. Probably."

"And of course," added Marzia, "we must acquire for you a Zolodrev seed."

Tim touched the brim of his hat. "Thank you. Truly." Turning to Zazila and Zilili, he pressed his hand to where Zazila's heart might have been. "And thank you, ladies—for the walk, for the half, for tomorrow, whenever it begins."

Zazila drifted to his side with a glow that would have lit a larger room.

Zilili smiled faintly. "We shall see."

A few minutes later, the family guided Tim up through a sloping tunnel toward the Zolodrev tree, the guards, and Viola. The earth pressed cool around him, carrying the faint echo of voices and the scent of garlic and possibility.

Chapter 29

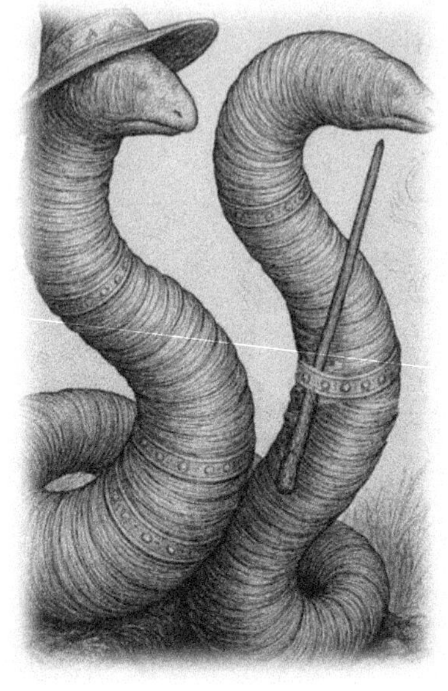

The earth beside the hedge trembled. A ringed head emerged, then another, then several more in stately procession. The Zuzzuzian worm-wizards rose from the soil with ceremonial slowness, gleaming with jewellery and dignity.

Viola's hand found Pall's shoulder. "Tim," she breathed.

The locust appeared last, perched proudly between two elegant worm heads. He waved both front legs.

"Tim!" Viola scrambled forward, heedless of the wet grass. "We were so worried. You were gone so long we feared—"

Tim clicked rapidly, cutting her off. He straightened his hat and puffed his chest in a way that suggested he had news of great importance.

"Something did indeed happen," he began in Locus, "but there's no time for that now." He gestured grandly to his companions. "Viola, these are the

Zuzzuzian worm-wizards King Uhm spoke of. Allow me to introduce Huzzan Zuzzat, greatest of the worm-wizards; Marzia Brazia, witches of fine potion-craft; and Zazila Zilili, my… betrothed."

He delivered this last word with the solemn pride of one announcing royalty.

The humans heard only buzzing, clicks, and a scratchy sound like boots on gravel.

Viola blinked. Pall tilted his head. Johnson leaned forward politely, as if comprehension might arrive through sheer courtesy.

Silence stretched. Tim's antennae drooped.

The worms exchanged glances. Huzzan wore enough gold bands to alarm a jeweller and a pointed hat that listed to one side. Beside him, Zuzzat brandished a wand so long it threatened to poke his neighbour. The matriarchs, Marzia and Brazia, glittered in filigree and carried between them a portable cauldron no larger than a purse.

"Well?" Zazila whispered. "Aren't they going to respond?"

"How rude," murmured Zilili.

"Really!" Zazila's rings jingled with indignation. "And this is the *extraordinary* Viola?"

Tim's antennae shot straight up. "Oh no. Oh no, no, no."

"What is it?" asked Huzzan.

"I forgot," Tim groaned. "They can't understand me. They're… surface folk."

"Ah," said Zuzzat. "Limited in the head."

Marzia sighed. "Dear boy, leave it to us. We speak a dozen languages, including Human Common."

Huzzan cleared his throat. "Good evening, human child. I am Huzzan, sorcerer supreme."

"We are sorcerer supreme," corrected Zuzzat.

"Pay no attention to the men, dearie," said Marzia. "It's us ladies you'll want to get to know."

"Our magic is much more reliable," added Brazia.

"Talking worms!" Viola whispered, eyes wide. "Tim, you found them! Are you really worm-wizards?"

"Of course," said Huzzan, mildly offended. He had worn his most impressive hat precisely for this.

"I'm so glad to make your acquaintance," Viola said, managing a curtsey despite the wet grass. "King Uhm told us of you. You're our only hope."

The worms' demeanour softened at once. Even Zazila, who had been prepared to dislike this human girl intensely, found herself somewhat charmed.

"Manners," Brazia observed. "One so rarely finds them above ground."

"Now then," said Zuzzat, "to business. You wish to shrink. We can arrange that."

Viola's face lit. "Truly? You can make me small enough to meet the Queen of the Brean?"

"Of course," said Marzia. "We are worm-wizards. Growing, shrinking—it's all the same principle."

"But shrinking is delicate," warned Huzzan. "It demands the strongest enchantment. One miscalculation and—"

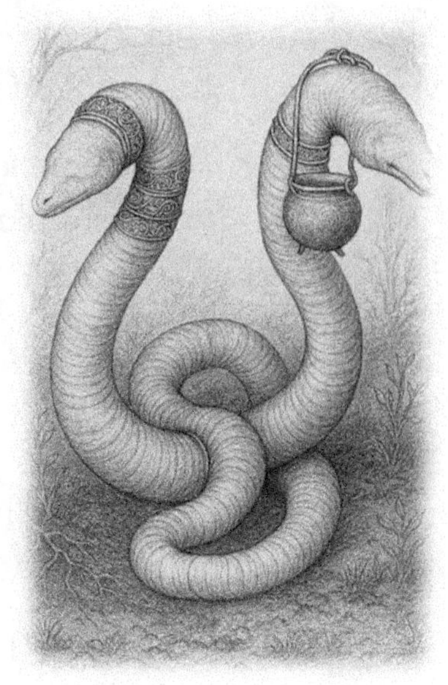

"Rubbish," said Brazia. "The men always claim difficulty to feel important. A solid potion will do."

"A potion alone is insufficient," protested Zuzzat. "The spell must be woven through—"

"The spell will unravel without proper ingredients—"

"Shhh!" Viola pressed her palms together, glancing toward the guards. "Please. Someone might hear you."

The worms fell silent, chastened.

"Very well," said Zuzzat. "We shall combine methods. The women brew, the men enchant. Double the art, double the result."

"Or double the explosion," muttered Pall.

Marzia tapped his shoe with a ringed coil. "Such faith warms the heart, young man."

Tim scraped a small circle in the dirt with one leg. "Before we discuss shrinking," he said quietly, "they need to know the truth."

Then Tim told Viola the tale, and the worms translated: how, after three years, the ravening hunger overtook every locust; how the Zolodrev fruit could calm it; how their queen had come to this very tree only to be refused by the Czar.

Viola's hands clenched. "That's why she's in hiding," she murmured. "Not because she abandoned them— because she failed."

"The fruit can stop it," Tim said. "But we have no tree. So I'm going to steal a seed."

"Tim, no—" Viola began.

"Yes," he said firmly. "My people are dying. I'm dying. In a year, maybe less, I'll become what everyone fears. Unless we grow our own Zolodrev."

"Then we'll help you," said Viola. Her mind was already racing. "We'll need a distraction. A way under the fence. Someone small enough to…" She stopped. "The shrinking potion."

"The tree is guarded," Johnson said. "Four soldiers, four dogs. They are ordered to stare in every direction and raise the alarm at once."

"Four guards," Viola repeated. "Johnson, when do they change shifts?"

"Tenth bell. One hour."

"And during the change?"

"Eight, briefly. Distracted by reports."

"Then we go during the change," Viola said. "Huzzan, can you tunnel beneath the fence?"

"Child, we are worms. We excel in under."

"Good. Johnson, distract them. Keep their attention on the tree."

Johnson frowned. "How would I distract eight armed soldiers?"

"Ask about the tree," said Viola. "How many fruits it bears. Its pattern of growth. The seasonal variation."

"Why would they—" Pall began.

"Because Johnson is Molgorodian," said Viola. "And Molgorodians can turn any topic into a very long conversation. No offence, Johnson."

"None taken," he said. "Though I would be genuinely interested in the answer."

"Perfect," said Viola. "Keep them talking."

"And then?" asked Zazila.

"Then someone climbs the tree and takes a seed," said Viola, staring up at the Zolodrev. Even in the rain it loomed magnificent, its branches spread like a crown. "I'll go. I'm light, and once I'm shrunk—"

"No," said Pall.

She turned to him.

"No," he repeated. "You're too important. The elves gave me a sword for bravery. I think they meant this." He touched the wooden rapier at his side.

"But you've never climbed—"

"I've come this far," Pall said. "And if there's one thing I've learned from you, it's that you never say I can't. Even when it seems impossible. You don't give up. And I won't either."

Viola studied him. The hunched boy who saw the worst in everything was gone. Rain ran down his hair and over the set line of his jaw.

"All right," she said softly. "You'll climb."

"But how will he lower the fruit without noise?" asked Marzia. "The branches rustle. The fruit thuds."

Tim lifted a coil of faintly shining thread. "We use this."

The worms inhaled as one.

"Hesperides silk!" Marzia breathed. "However did you—"

"Never mind how he acquired it," said Zuzzat. "It is exactly what we need."

"I knew he was a hero the moment I saw him," Huzzan declared, forgetting entirely how he had first met Tim.

Zazila wiggled closer to Tim. "So resourceful," she sighed.

Zilili gave her sister a look.

"So," Viola said briskly, "the plan. At the tenth bell, Johnson approaches the guards during their change and keeps them talking. While they're distracted, the worms tunnel beneath the fence. Pall and I drink the potion and shrink. We crawl through the tunnel. Pall climbs, ties the silk to a fruit, cuts it free, and lowers it down. We catch it and pull it underground before anyone notices."

"It's mad," said Zilili.

"It's brilliant," said Zazila.

"It's dangerous," added Marzia. "If the potion is wrong, you could shrink to nothing."

"If we don't try," said Viola quietly, "Tim's people will never be saved. And mine will starve."

A silence followed. Somewhere in the distance, a dog barked.

Everyone froze. Footsteps crunched on gravel. The sound grew close, then faded again.

Marzia spoke first. "We must begin. The potion needs time to brew."

"And the enchantment must be layered carefully," said Huzzan.

"Already in hand," said Brazia. "Marzia, the reduction salts."

The worms bent to their work. The tiny cauldron appeared. Powders and herbs were drawn from hidden rings. Marzia and Brazia began to chant while Huzzan and Zuzzat traced glowing sigils in the air.

Viola watched them work, her mind spinning through contingencies. What if the potion wore off underground? What if the guards noticed? What if—

"Viola," Tim said softly, climbing onto her knee. She could not understand the words, but she understood the tone.

"You're not monsters," she said. "You're just hungry."

The tenth bell would ring soon. And then they would attempt the greatest theft in the history of Molgorosk—or die trying.

"It will work," Viola said, more to herself than to anyone else.

"It will be the greatest theft of all time," Zazila declared.

"Or we'll be caught and executed," Zilili allowed.

Pall turned pale but nodded.

The worms resumed their humming magic. The cauldron bubbled. The rain whispered through the leaves.

And in the distance, faint and far, the bell began to chime.

The garden went still but for the rain—and the small, steady pulse of hope.

Chapter 30

The bell tolled its first note across Molgorosk, deep and heavy.

One. The changing of the guard had begun.

"It's ready!" Marzia announced, though the cauldron still fizzed ominously.

"Nearly ready," Brazia corrected. "The enchantment needs another—"

"There's no time!" Huzzan hissed. "The guards are coming!"

Through the hedge, Viola glimpsed figures approaching in neat formation. Four new soldiers marched toward the tree, boots splashing through puddles. The old guard stirred from their posts, preparing their report.

Dong! Two.

"Is it safe?" Pall whispered, staring at the thimble-sized cauldron where the liquid shifted between purple and green.

"Safe?" Zuzzat stroked his beard-rings thoughtfully. "Define safe."

"It's rising beautifully," Marzia said. "Don't drink too much."

"How much is too much?" Viola asked. "There's barely anything there."

"Half each," said Brazia. "No more."

"But how do we measure half in a thimble?"

Three.

The worms erupted into argument.

"Just drink it quick and trust the magic!" said Huzzan.

"No, careful sips!" said Zuzzat. "The dosage is critical!"

"Oh, for soil's sake," Marzia muttered. "Humans—so particular about measurements."

Pall's hands trembled. "I have a bad feeling about this."

"You have a bad feeling about everything," Viola said gently. She picked up the tiny cauldron, warm against her palm. It smelled of earth and lightning and something that made her nose tingle.

Four.

"Now or never," she said.

She drank. The potion tasted like dirt and starlight, bitter and bright. She passed it to Pall.

He closed his eyes, muttered something like a prayer, and drank the rest.

Five.

Nothing happened.

"See?" Zuzzat snapped. "You zigged when you should have zagged!"

"My enchantment was perfect!" Huzzan shot back. "Your wand-tapping was faulty!"

"Maybe you drank it upside down?" Brazia wondered.

"All of you calm down," Marzia said. "Give it a moment!"

Then Viola felt it.

It began in her fingertips—a pulling, a great invisible hand stretching the world instead of her. The grass rose like towers. The hedge swelled. Raindrops crashed down as boulders of water.

"It's working," she breathed, her voice thin and high.

Pall grabbed her arm. His hand was shrinking too—or she was—or everything was. The ground rushed up. The worms, once small, now grew immense until they filled the sky.

When it stopped, Viola stood barely an inch tall. The grass loomed like a green forest. Each raindrop was a falling globe. The worms glittered like dragons of soil and jewellery.

"Never doubted it," Huzzan declared.

"Worked perfectly," said Zuzzat.

"Exactly as designed," Brazia added, having just argued otherwise.

Marzia preened. "You'll notice you can understand our Tim now. Special ingredient—language comprehension. Very advanced magic."

Tim hopped forward, clicking and scraping. "Viola! Can you hear me? Really hear me?"

"Tim!" She ran to him and threw her arms around his neck. "I can understand you!"

"Excuse me," said Zazila coolly, sliding between them. "That's my fiancé you're embracing."

"Your what?"

"Fiancé," repeated Zazila, coiling round Tim. "We're betrothed."

Pall blinked rainwater away. "Tim, you're getting married?"

"It's a long story—"

"No time!" boomed Huzzan, his voice like thunder now. "The guards! Look!"

Through the forest of grass, Viola saw movement: eight giants in armour, boots like cliffs, dogs the size of buildings sniffing the air.

Six. Halfway through the change.

"Go!" Marzia commanded. "We'll handle the tunnel!"

Johnson, bless him, was already moving. At full size, visible through the hedge, he strolled toward the guards with unhurried dignity.

"Good evening, gentlemen!" he called. "I have travelled from the country to admire the Czar's famous Zolodrev arboris. Might one inquire—purely academically—about its annual fruit yield per cubic rod?"

The worms plunged into the earth. They moved like thought, soil rippling behind them.

"This way!" Huzzan cried. "Under the fence!"

Viola and Pall ran. At this scale, every step was a leap. The grass parted like curtains. The air smelled of roots and Zolodrev spice.

The worms worked with astonishing speed, carving a tunnel wide enough for inch-tall travellers. Soon they reached the fence.

"The posts go deep," Zuzzat warned. "Deeper still!"

They descended into darkness. Viola felt Pall's hand find hers and squeeze. Above them Johnson's voice echoed faintly: "And what of drainage efficiency in clay soils versus loam?"

Light ahead—then space. They emerged beneath the roots of the Zolodrev. The vast wooden pillars arched above like the ribs of a cathedral. Through them glimmered the wet night sky.

"Here," said Huzzan. "We'll dig your exit by these roots, hidden from view."

The worms opened a small upward tunnel. Beyond it waited the grass and the colossal trunk.

Pall stared upward. To the first branch was twenty feet—at his size, a mountain.

"You can do this," Viola said.

Tim approached with the coil of Hesperides silk glowing faintly like moonlight made solid. He held it out.

For a heartbeat they only looked at each other. Then Tim extended one foreleg.

Pall shook it solemnly. The silk draped over his shoulder, light as air yet strong as steel.

"Thank you," Tim said. "For doing this. For my people."

"I know you can do it," Viola said softly. "I know you can."

Pall breathed once, twice—and climbed.

The bark rose before him like a cliff. Each ridge was a wall, each drop of rain a falling sea. The wood smelled of sap and spice. Far below,

Johnson's voice droned on: "—and according to Subsection 9 regarding imperial botany—"

Hand, foot, hand, foot.

The seventh bell tolled. The sky deepened to black. Stars winked through cloud.

A moth the size of a cart brushed past him, wings whispering like cloth. His arms burned. The tree stretched endlessly up. When he made the mistake of looking down, the world tilted. The ground was a dark ocean far below.

He froze. His breath came fast. *I can't do this.* The thought was calm, certain. *I'm not brave. I'm just Pall. I'll fall. I'll—*

He pressed his forehead to the bark. The roughness steadied him.

Below, Viola was watching. Tim was watching. All of them trusted him.

He thought of Viola, who never gave up. Of the elves who'd called him brave. Of Tim, who still believed in kindness.

He climbed again.

The first branch met him like a miracle. He rolled onto it, gasping. The branch was wide as a road. The fruits hung ahead—three golden cubes glowing faintly in the starlight, smelling of sweetness and rain.

He approached one. Pushed. It barely moved. Heavy as stone.

He uncoiled the Hesperides silk, tied it to a smaller branch above, looped the other end around the fruit's stem. The knot held.

If he simply cut the stem, the fruit would drop and tear free. He needed control.

He wound the silk several times to make a friction brake, testing the tension. It might work. Probably.

Below, dogs prowled. Their noses twitched. Guards shifted uneasily.

"The citizen appears to be loitering," one said.

"Discussing botany, Subsection 9," another replied.

"Carry on," said a third.

Pall drew his elven rapier. The living wood glowed faintly green-gold.

One swing.

The blade sliced through the stem. The fruit fell.

The silk caught it with a wrench that almost flung him off the branch. He gripped tight, arms screaming, and began lowering it hand over hand. The silk slid hot against his palms, the weight relentless.

Below, Johnson's lecture swelled: "—and naturally, pollination encourages the nocturnal moth, which sings at precisely this pitch—"

The nearest dog stopped and sniffed. Its great head turned toward the tree.

One guard followed its gaze. "Wait—did something move?"

Pall froze, clinging to the bark. Viola held her breath. The fruit hung motionless on the silk, glowing faintly like a captured star.

Another guard frowned. "I thought I saw—"

And that was when Johnson did something brave. Something heroic.

He sang.

He had never sung before. No one in Molgorod had. The very idea of melody had only just been introduced to Johnson that afternoon by Viola, and even then, only by accident.

He drew a deep, academic breath and produced a single note.

"Ooooooiiiiii!"

It was not quite in any key, nor entirely out of one. It began as a query, swelled into alarm, and finished somewhere between triumph and indigestion.

But it was loud. Astonishingly loud.

The dogs barked in confusion. The guards spun round.

"Citizen! Desist at once!"

Johnson broke into a jog, circling the tree like an enormous, tuneless comet.

"Stop! You are in violation of—of something!"

One guard tackled him. Two helped. A fourth began writing a ticket with deep concentration.

All backs were turned.

The golden fruit slid down the silk, silent as a dream. It reached the grass and vanished into the tunnel.

Viola caught its glowing side, guiding it into the earth. It was like catching the moon. The fruit sank out of sight.

Pall glanced once at the silk still tied above. "Sorry," he whispered to it, then seized the line and slid down.

The guards released Johnson with a warning and a fine. He ambled away, humming cheerfully. None noticed the faint gleam high in the branches or the tiny shape that dropped into the grass and vanished underground.

Viola's hands pulled Pall inside. Behind them, the worms worked fast, closing the tunnel. The soil rippled and stilled, leaving no trace.

In the dark, damp air, Viola found Pall's hand and squeezed it.

They had done it.

Under eight guards, eight dogs, and a dozen foolish arguments, they had stolen life itself from the Czar's garden.

Chapter 31

he fruit glowed in the darkness—golden and warm, as if the sun had been folded into a cube and wrapped in honeyed skin.

"It's beautiful," Viola breathed.

"It's *enormous*," said Pall. At their current size it was twice his height and nearly filled the chamber.

"Magnificent," Zuzzat declared, his rings chiming as he circled it. "Absolutely magnificent." He inhaled as if the air itself were magic.

"Not a single blemish," said Huzzan, prodding the skin with one ringed segment.

"Just as I predicted," murmured Brazia.

"You predicted?" said Marzia. "I seem to recall—"

"Could we perhaps focus," Pall said mildly, "on how we're meant to eat something the size of a room?"

Tim clicked forward, antennae quivering. "I can help with that!"

"My brave fiancé will open it," purred Zazila, her rings glinting.

"He will not," said Zilili. "Let the human warrior carve it."

"Warrior?" Pall said, looking around for one.

Viola cut in. "You did the impossible, and you have the only sword."

He sighed, stepped up, and raised the blade.

The skin parted like silk. A sweet, sharp scent filled the air—spice and rain and sunlight layered together.

"Oh my," whispered Marzia.

Pall sliced again, cutting out a section. The flesh glowed orange fading to rose, shot with golden veins that pulsed faintly. Each cut released more perfume until the air shimmered with it.

Viola lifted a piece. It was warm in her hands. She glanced at Pall; he nodded.

Together they bit down.

The taste struck like lightning. Hotter than pricklepepper—Viola's eyes watered—then the sweetness rolled in, honey over flame. The flesh was chewy, and with each bite came a sound:

Snap. Pop.

With every snap a warmth spread through her, not in her stomach but in her chest—a lightness, a strange peace.

Pall's eyes were closed. Tears streaked his face.

"Are you all right?" she whispered.

"I'm happy," he said simply. "I don't think I've ever been happy."

Tim made a sound like a bell, pure and ringing. "I don't think I've ever not been hungry!"

The fruit did not end. It chewed like gum that never lost its flavour.

"We can't eat all this," Viola said around the chewy wad in her mouth.

"Of course not," said Marzia softly. "We'll prepare it to go."

"And for study," added Zuzzat.

Snap. Pop. The air hummed with contentment.

At last Pall turned back to the fruit. In its heart, where the stem had joined, he found a seed—small, grey, hard as stone, shaped like a perfect brick.

He cut it free and held it out.

Tim stepped forward, trembling, and received it as one might receive hope itself. "Thank you," he whispered.

"It's beautiful," sighed Zazila, stroking the seed.

"No it isn't," said Zilili. "It's rough and lumpy."

"Beauty isn't everything," Viola said carefully.

"That's what people say," Zazila sniffed, "when they're not the beautiful one."

But Zazila had already coiled round Tim again. "We'll plant it together, darling. Just the two of us. The greatest tree that ever grew."

Tim's antennae flickered with something between joy and panic.

"We're not safe yet," Pall said quietly. "We still have to escape Molgorosk."

The warm, sweet air cooled.

"At this size," Viola said, "a rat could kill us. How long does the shrinking last?"

A silence.

"It's permanent," said Zuzzat.

"Should wear off in a year or two," said Huzzan. "Three at most."

"About an hour," declared Brazia.

"Depends how you feel," suggested Marzia.

Viola stared at them. "But at this size it will take forever to reach the Queen."

"Tut-tut," said Huzzan. "You won't be *walking*."

"What?"

"You'll fly, of course!"

The chamber froze.

"Fly," Pall repeated. "Did you say *fly*?"

"On birds!" Huzzan said brightly. "Fastest way to travel at your scale. Perfectly safe."

"Daddy, no!" cried Zazila. "Teleport us instead!"

"Too dangerous," said Zuzzat. "The seed would likely explode."

"As would you," added Brazia.

Zazila paled—or would have, had worms much colour to lose.

"Can we trust them?" Zilili asked. "Birds are… they're…" She trailed off.

"There are matters even larger than war," Zuzzat said.

Viola frowned. "War?"

"Oh yes," said Huzzan. "Terrible business. Much pecking."

"And eating," added Brazia.

"They eat us," said Zilili flatly. "Alive."

"Not *all* birds," protested Marzia. "Just most."

"I'm not doing it," said Zazila, coiling tight. "They'll eat me. I'm far too *beautiful* to be eaten."

"You're too *vain* to be eaten," muttered Zilili.

"This is madness," said Pall. "You expect us to ride creatures that devour you?"

"Not from malice," said Zuzzat. "From diet."

"That doesn't help!"

"We've arranged safe passage," said Huzzan. "Or rather, we're *arranging* it. Negotiations are ongoing."

"Ongoing?" said Viola.

"Delicate," said Marzia.

"Uncertain," said Brazia.

"Probably doomed," said Zilili.

Tim looked up from the seed. "I'll go," he said quietly.

Zazila recoiled. "No! You'll be eaten!"

"If that's what it takes to save my people," said Tim, "then I'll risk it."

Zilili made a sound like respect.

Zazila made one like despair.

Viola stepped beside him. "We'll all go together. We'll keep each other safe."

"Together," said Pall, though he looked like he might be sick.

"Well," said Zuzzat. "That's settled."

"Not settled," Zazila hissed.

"Decidedly unsettled," muttered Zilili.

And somewhere ahead, Viola thought, lay a journey stranger than any before.

They had stolen from the Czar. They had shrunk to the size of insects. They had tasted magic itself.

Now they would fly.

She met Pall's eyes. Neither said what both felt—that they were terrified, that it was impossible, and that they would do it anyway.

In the damp earth beneath Molgorosk, with a stolen seed, a fading spell, and a plan that might end in disaster, they began to prepare for the most perilous journey of all.

Chapter 32

he tunnel opened into the wet night. Viola and Pall stepped out beneath the hedge, still scarcely an inch tall.

Johnson was waiting. When he noticed movement in the grass, he approached with the careful gravity of someone afraid to crush a miracle. The ground trembled as he knelt. His hand descended like a drawbridge until it lay flat against the earth.

Viola looked at Pall.

Pall looked at the hand.

"It's a long way up," he said.

"You've climbed higher," Viola answered, thinking of the Zolodrev.

They climbed onto his palm. The ground fell away; the garden spread beneath them like a map. The hedge became a forest. The rain became a sea of falling worlds, each drop vast enough to drown them.

Up close, Johnson's face was a landscape—valleys and ridges, skin textured like ploughed fields. But his eyes were kind.

"Thank you!" Viola called, cupping her hands.

His whisper was still thunder. "Did you get it?"

"Yes! We saved a piece for you!"

Johnson shook his head—tectonic, deliberate. "I cannot. It is a crime to eat the Zolodrev fruit."

"Are you sure? You'd never be hungry again."

"That would be beneficial," he admitted. "But my neighbours would grow suspicious. And the penalty is severe. Much greater than a ticket."

"Your country has too many bad laws," Pall called up.

"Laws are not bad," Johnson said. "They simply are. Like rain."

"Not everywhere," Pall persisted. "In my country, you can drive your cart anywhere you like."

Johnson frowned faintly. "But why would you drive where the line is not efficient?"

"Because it's fun," Viola said. "You might find something special. Like a Molgorodian who's kind."

"I am not special." His voice was calm. "Kindness is not practical. It is just something in me that has never been corrected."

Rain pattered against his hat.

"Will you stay this size forever?" he asked.

"No one knows."

"That seems unsafe. Did they not test the spell first?"

"Worms don't test," Pall said. "They just… happen."

"What will you do now?"

"We still have to find the Queen of the Brean," said Viola. "But now we can help her—and Dampenia too."

Johnson nodded slowly. "I could take you."

"That's kind," Viola said, "but the worm-wizards will bargain with the birds to fly us."

"Not clear we won't be eaten," Pall muttered.

"Flight would be quickest," Johnson reasoned. "But if you grew mid-journey, you would fall."

Pall blanched. "I hadn't thought of that. Perhaps the cart—"

"We'll take our chances," Viola said. Her tone closed the subject.

She looked up at Johnson's vast face. "Johnson?"

"Yes?"

"I'll miss you."

He blinked, puzzled. "Will you be striking me?"

Viola laughed. "No. It means I'll be sad not to see you. I wish you could come."

"I am too large to ride a bird."

"You could visit Dampenia," she said quickly. "When all this is over."

Pall added, "You could study our roads. No coloured lines."

Johnson was silent a long time. The rain whispered around them.

"That could be educational," he said at last. "Perhaps there is a visa. I would require a farm-caretaker permit. Yes. Possible."

From the distance came the beating of wings—many wings—slicing through the rain.

"Johnson," Viola said, "we must go. The birds are coming for the meeting."

He looked up. "Interesting. I must also leave the gardens before I am fined again."

"How many tickets now?" she asked.

Johnson drew a sheaf of papers from his coat. Even from her height, she saw the official seals.

He read in his steady voice: "Loitering after eighth bell. Failure to proceed directly along designated walkway. Unsanctioned botanical inquiry. Disturbing the peace through unapproved vocalization. Providing incorrect documentation. Standing in rain without permit—"

"What? There's a *permit* for rain?"

"For standing in it. One must have purpose."

"That's insane."

"It is regulation." He folded the papers neatly. "This brings my annual total to forty-seven."

"Forty-seven!"

"It is not large. Some reach hundreds."

The wingbeats grew louder. Dark shapes crossed the sky.

"We have to let you go," Viola said.

Pall bowed on the giant palm. "Thank you, Johnson. You were braver than you think."

Johnson looked faintly confused but nodded.

Viola stepped forward. "Could you bring me closer? To your cheek?"

The world tilted. His face loomed, vast and warm. Viola leaned in and pressed her lips to his skin.

He froze.

Then he lifted her back to eye level. "Why did you press your lips on me?"

"It means I love you."

A long silence. Rain fell softly between them.

"What is love?" Johnson asked.

Viola smiled, though her eyes were wet. "I'll teach you when you visit."

"I look forward to learning," he said. "Yes. Visiting your country would be productive."

Gently, he lowered his hand. The grass rose around them like trees. Viola, Pall, and Tim stepped onto the wet earth.

Johnson stood to his full height. "Good evening," he said.

Pall grinned. "Johnson! You just spoke without purpose."

For the first time, Johnson smiled—small, uncertain, but real. "I did. You said 'good morning' earlier. Now it is evening. Was that correct?"

"Yes," Pall said. "Perfect."

Johnson began to turn away.

"Johnson!" Viola called.

He paused. "Yes?"

"I liked your song."

The smile widened, shy but sure. "I liked it as well."

"How did it feel?"

He hesitated, searching for language. When it came, it was quiet and slow.

"It felt like standing in rain without a permit," he said. "But not caring. Like choosing an inefficient route because the view is interesting."

He stopped there, words exhausted.

Viola pressed a hand to her heart. "That's beautiful," she whispered, though he could not hear her.

Johnson nodded once, formal again. Then he turned and walked away into the rain, his footsteps fading like distant thunder.

Chapter 33

The worms led them beneath a forgotten stone bench where moss grew like carpet and rain pooled in old cracks.

"Remember," said Huzzan, his rings chiming with each word. "Birds cannot be trusted."

"Absolutely not," said Zuzzat.

"Never," added Brazia.

"Well," began Marzia, "sometimes—"

"Never," the others chorused.

Viola sat cross-legged on a pebble beside Pall and Tim. Zazila coiled round Tim's arm while Zilili tried to look brave.

"You must not tell them where the Queen of the Brean lives," said Huzzan. "They would camp there and feed until not a locust remained."

"And under no circumstances," said Zuzzat, leaning close, rings trembling near Viola's nose, "tell them about the Zolodrev seed."

"Why?" asked Pall.

"They'll steal it," said Brazia. "Birds are thieves. Elegant, feathered thieves."

"Then why meet them at all?" Viola asked.

"Because," said Marzia gently, "we need them. And they know it."

A shadow passed overhead. Then another. The measured beat of wings filled the air—calm, deliberate, and full of ownership.

Three birds descended.

The first was a budgie, elderly and dignified, plumage faded from bright blue to grey-green. He wore glasses, and several rows of medals hung from his chest. The second, a mockingbird—sleek and silver-throated—moved as though the air were hers by law. Behind them came a chickadee, bright-eyed and bouncing, who couldn't seem to stop looking at everything at once.

"Ambassador Chip," said the budgie crisply. "Fluent in Human Common, Insect Common, Bird Cant, and seventeen dialects. At your service." He bowed.

"Madame Glint," said the mockingbird, admiring herself in a raindrop. "Of the Northern Glints. Surely you've heard of us."

"Can't say we have," murmured Pall.

Madame Glint heard and looked shocked.

"Shall we begin?" Huzzan asked stiffly.

Chip planted a white feather in the soil. "The flag of truce," he said. "Valid until sunrise or agreement, whichever arrives first."

"Agreed," said Zuzzat.

"Now." Chip adjusted his glasses. "The worms propose safe transport for two humans, one Brean locust, and two worm juveniles to the entrance of the Barrowmere."

"Entrance only," Brazia cut in. "We're not saying what happens after."

Madame Glint laughed, like knives in wind chimes. "We don't care where they go. We care what we're paid."

"You'll be compensated fairly," Marzia said.

"Fairly." Glint smoothed a wing. "Two worms per season. Your choice which."

Silence. Then Huzzan's rings rattled like storm bells. "You'd have us sacrifice our own? Barbaric."

"Seems fair to me," Glint said. "Or you could walk."

"This is outrageous!" Zuzzat flared.

"Perhaps another form of payment can be discussed," Chip suggested mildly.

Huzzan took a steadying breath. "Other considerations, then."

The real negotiation began.

Marzia argued for goodwill between earth and sky; Brazia listed bird betrayals. Glint yawned. Chip reminded them that the worms had called the session and must expect to pay. Zuzzat muttered about "avian tyranny." Huzzan and Zuzzat paced, sometimes in opposite directions.

After hours of argument, Chip summarized:

"For transport and safety to the Barrowmere entrance, the Zuzzuzian worms agree to—

"One: abstain from enchanting any bird's nest for one migration."

"Agreed," said Huzzan.

"Two: remain deeper than ten feet underground for half a season."

"Excessive," Brazia snapped.

"Agreed," Zuzzat said through clenched segments.

"Three: forego protective magic for a quarter season."

"You'd leave us defenceless," said Marzia.

"You can pay less and have safe passage only halfway," Glint replied.

"Agreed," Marzia sighed."

Chip was making final notes when, with a cruel smile, Madame Glint added, "And we want the secret of your shrinking magic."

"Never!" all four worms cried. "That knowledge is sacred!"

Even the ambassador looked startled. "Madame …"

"Then we have no deal," said Glint.

Rain fell softly. The feather drooped under its weight.

Viola's hand went to her pocket—and found something small and round, shaped rather like an egg. "What do I have in my pocket?" she wondered aloud. She'd carried it all this way and had completely forgotten until this moment.

King Uhm's gift.

She drew it out. Even shrunk to the size of a thimble, it was breathtaking—a jewelled egg that seemed to hold all the colours of dawn, wrapped in golden filigree like morning frost.

"Wait," she said quietly.

Everyone turned.

She held up the egg. "Would this help?"

Chip's glasses slid down his beak. Glint gasped. The chickadee bounced forward, wide-eyed.

"That is royal treasure," Chip whispered.

"It was a gift from King Uhm of the Talpan," Viola said.

"Viola," Pall warned, "you promised to deliver it to Queen Isiiala."

"I know," she said. "But we must reach her first."

"That single gem," Chip murmured, "could buy flight to the ends of the earth."

"Then we have a deal?" Viola asked.

"Of course not," said Glint lightly. "We'll take the egg and the other terms."

"What!" Zuzzat exploded. "Skyway robbery!"

"Professional standards," Glint corrected.

"You have *greed* to maintain," Brazia spat.

Chip looked uneasy. "Given the egg's value, perhaps some reduction—"

"No reductions," Glint said firmly.

"But madam, the value clearly—"

"No. Reductions."

Chip sighed. "Very well. But in recognition of the human's offer, the Bird Kingdom will name her an honoured ally—protected wherever wings can reach."

"That's kind," said Viola.

"It's politics," Glint said. "We look good, you get a title, everyone wins." She paused. "Except the worms, of course."

"This is exploitation," Zuzzat growled.

"Cultural exchange," Chip corrected. "The egg will rest in the Grand Rookery Museum for all to admire."

"You'll never sell it?" Brazia demanded.

"Never," said Chip. "It will be treasured."

"Unlike worms," Zilili muttered.

"Unlike worms who violate treaties," Glint said. "We keep our word. Ask anyone."

"I can't," Brazia replied. "You ate them."

Glint's eyes glittered. "Dietary accidents. This is diplomacy."

The worms held a silent conference of rings and sighs. Then Huzzan said, "We accept."

"Excellent." Chip marked his ledger. "By authority of the High Council of Wings, under witness of earth and sky, we declare these terms binding until completion or death."

He hopped forward. Zuzzat slid to meet him. They both spat on the ground—one clear, one luminous.

"Sealed," they said together.

Viola blinked. "That's how you seal treaties?"

"Of course," said the chickadee brightly.

"Appalling," Pall muttered.

"Authentic," the chickadee said.

The treaty was struck.

The worms gathered round Tim, Zazila, and Zilili. Marzia wept softly, rings chiming.

"My beautiful girls," she said. "Be safe. Distrust any bird that smiles."

"That's all birds," Zilili said thickly.

"Exactly."

Huzzan cleared his throat. "You've got good sense, Zilili. Keep your sister from doing anything too decorative."

"I'll try."

"And Zazila," he added, "beauty means nothing if you're eaten."

"That's terrible advice!" she wailed.

Zuzzat faced Tim solemnly. "You carry hope for your people. Few creatures bear such weight. But I think you will."

Tim's antennae trembled. "Thank you, Master Zuzzat."

"Call me father." Zuzzat's rings clinked softly. "You're also family now."

Huzzan added, "Get the other half won, son."

"I'll try."

Brazia turned to Viola and Pall. "You did better than expected. Try not to die; it would complicate matters."

"We'll do our best," said Viola.

One by one, they said their farewells—tears and rings and promises to reunite when the world was less impossible.

Before departure, Marzia and Brazia packed what remained of the Zolodrev fruit—carefully sliced, wrapped in leaf, and sealed with wax—so the children could carry it to the starving Brean. "A gift for your Queen," Marzia said. "Let her see that even worms can share light."

Lieutenant Chirrup bounced forward, brimming with energy.

"Hello! Hi! I'm your pilot! Madame Glint takes the worms and locust; I take you two. Thrilling, yes?"

"Utterly," Pall said faintly.

Viola took his hand.

Chirrup spun in a small circle. "Oh, this is going to be such fun! I've never carried humans before!"

Chip approached, holding the jewelled egg wrapped in spider-silk. "This will be honoured," he said gravely. "And you, Viola of Dampenia, are under avian protection."

"Thank you," she said.

Madame Glint called, "Are we leaving or composing speeches?"

"Coming!" Chirrup crouched. "Climb on—just behind my head. Hold the feathers; they're stronger than they look."

Viola and Pall exchanged the familiar look that meant *this is absurd but necessary.* They climbed onto the chickadee's back. His feathers were warm and surprisingly soft, each one thick as a rope at their size. Viola found a good grip. Pall wrapped his arms around her waist.

"Ready?" Chirrup asked.

"No," Pall said.

"Perfect."

The wings struck once—thunder in silk. Again—and the ground fell away.

The garden dwindled: bench to monument, hedge to forest, worms to glimmer. Rain streamed past like rivers.

Higher.

The gate guards became toys. The Zolodrev a stick. Molgorosk spread like a rain-lit map.

Higher still.

Then there was only the sky—vast and rain-bright and full of impossible journeys—and the beating wings carrying them north toward whatever waited next.

"Magnificent, isn't it?" Chirrup cried into the wind. "Only—don't slip. The landing's dreadful."

"Comforting," Pall said through his teeth.

Viola laughed—clear, wild, and small against the storm—because they were flying, truly flying, and the world below was terrible and beautiful all at once.

The wings beat like heartbeats. The rain sang. And three tiny travellers rose into the night, carrying hope the size of a seed.

Chapter 34

Landing was less graceful than take-off.

Madame Glint dropped like a stone, pulling up at the last moment and scattering Tim, Zazila, and Zilili into the grass.

"You did that on purpose," Zilili said, spitting grass.

Glint shook her feathers. "Delivery complete without a peck. The Bird Kingdom keeps its word."

Lieutenant Chirrup landed with bouncing enthusiasm. "Magnificent! Did you feel the wind and rain? I've never carried humans before—did I mention that? Oh, I did? Well, it bears repeating!"

Viola slid off, legs wobbling. Pall followed, looking faintly green.

"Thank you," Viola managed. "Truly. You saved us days of travel."

"Think nothing of it!" Chirrup chirped. "If you ever need transport again, just whistle!"

Ambassador Chip arrived last, calm despite the rain. "The treaty is fulfilled. The jewelled egg will be displayed with honour. And you, Viola of Dampenia, are under avian protection."

"I'm very grateful," Viola said.

"Good," Glint added. "Now I have important matters to attend." She flew off.

"Goodbye!" cried Chirrup. "Good luck! Don't get eaten! Oh, that's awful—don't get killed! No, good luck! That's better!" And he too was gone.

Chip lingered. "A word of advice: the Brean Queen is bitter and angry. Choose your words carefully."

"We will," Viola said.

The birds rose into the grey sky until even Chirrup's chatter was gone.

Zazila uncurled slowly, rings chiming with relief. "I thought she was going to eat us, treaty or no."

"She considered it," Zilili said.

Tim adjusted his hat. "Well. That's over."

"You were brave," Viola said to Pall.

"I was sick," Pall replied.

Viola checked her satchel. The packets of Zolodrev fruit—wrapped in leaf and wax by Marzia and Brazia—were still glowing faintly. "At least the gift survived," she said. "For the Queen's people."

The Barrowmere entrance yawned before them—dark, damp, and, now that they were small, enormous. Slowly they went down. The light faded. Roots thickened overhead.

Viola noticed something strange: she could still see. Not well, but enough to make out shapes, edges, the tunnel's curve.

"Pall," she whispered. "Can you see?"

"I… yes. A little. How?"

"Mother's shrinking potion," Zilili said over her shoulder. "Night vision is a known side effect."

"Useful," Pall said.

"Very," Zilili agreed.

A deep shuffle echoed ahead. The tunnel trembled. Then a sniff.

"Halt!" said a low voice.

"Who goes there?" said another, higher one.

They could see them this time.

"We could just sneak by," Pall whispered. "We can see in the dark now."

"We're not sneaking past friends," Viola said firmly. "Humhum? Numni?"

A snuffle like a windstorm answered as Humhum's nose appeared. "Viola? You're back? And you're... very small. You found the worm-wizards!"

"Yes. Let me introduce the Zuzzuzian ladies, Zazila and Zilili. They're here to help the Queen."

"Enchanted," said Zazila.

"Don't mention it," said Zilili.

The sisters bowed.

"Well, that is something," Humhum said. "I guess you'll be wanting to go to the Queen's castle. Are you sure? The locusts aren't... what you'd call friendly."

"My people are cursed, hated, and mistreated everywhere," Tim said. "It tends to make one grumpy."

"True enough," Humhum allowed. His voice brightened. "Listen—we can help. The underground river's not far. We could carry you there. Save you hours of walking."

"That's incredibly kind," Viola said.

"Climb on, then," Humhum said, lowering himself to all fours."

His back was broad as a field. Viola and Pall climbed up, settling between his shoulder blades. Tim, Zazila, and Zilili found secure spots in his fur.

"Hold tight," Humhum warned.

The journey was swift and strange—a rolling, purposeful gait that covered ground impossibly fast. The tunnels blurred past. Viola pressed close to Pall, both of them clinging to the thick fur.

"Did the King give you that promotion?" Viola called.

"Not exactly," Humhum said.

"Not yet," Numni added.

"He's considering it," Humhum said carefully. "Very strongly."

"After we provide decades of loyal service," Numni finished.

"So—progress?" Pall suggested.

"Exactly," Humhum said. "Everyone's jealous, but we try not to brag."

They rode through the sloping chambers until the tunnels opened into a cavern so vast Viola forgot to breathe.

Lichens covered every surface, glowing soft green, blue, and gold. They dripped from stalactites and carpeted the walls in living light. A narrow river ran through the middle—black, swift, and dangerous, crowned with white spray. A bridge of fitted stone arched across it, its posts capped with softly glowing crystals.

"It's beautiful," Viola whispered.

"Don't fall in," Numni said. "You'd be swept away in seconds."

Humhum knelt, and they climbed down.

"You sure about this?" he asked.

"We have to try," Viola said.

"Then good luck," Numni said. "And be careful."

"We'll be careful," Pall promised.

"Goodbye, friends," Viola said.

The moles turned, padding back into darkness. Viola watched them go, then turned to face the bridge.

They crossed. Tim marched ahead, the seed stowed in his pack. Viola followed, hoping against hope that this would work. Then Pall, thinking of all the ways it could go horribly wrong. And last, Zazila and Zilili, murmuring words that might have been spells—or pep talks to keep their spirits up.

Each stone was cold and wet underfoot. Spray chilled their faces. The water rushed beneath the bridge. Pall looked down once and went pale.

"Bad idea," Viola said, pulling him back.

"Now you tell me."

At last they reached the far side. The passage beyond breathed with sound and scent—clicks, chitter, the sharp smell of iron.

Shapes stirred ahead. Locusts. Dozens. Armoured, scarred, hostile. Their mandibles gleamed. Their eyes were hard.

A commander stepped forward, spear lowered. "State your business."

Tim answered proudly. "We seek the Queen."

"The Queen sees no one."

"We bring a gift. A seed of hope."

A harsh laugh, clicking and cruel. "Hope? There is no hope."

They were surrounded instantly.

"How dare you—!" began Zilili, but Tim raised a hand for peace.

The commander circled them. "What do we have here? A locust, two worm-wizards, and two small humans—with Molgorodian stink on them."

Tim did not back down. "Yes. Many of us have come together. We've fought and risked our lives and done the impossible. The Queen would not want us turned away."

The commander hesitated, then said, "You want the Queen? Fine. We'll take you to her. She can decide your fate."

The soldiers moved in behind them, spears at their backs.

"Pall," Viola whispered.

"I know. Keep walking."

The walls turned from soil to smooth amber resin, glowing faintly as they widened into a hall. The Queen's palace rose before them—an amber cathedral of spirals and pillars, alive with golden light. At its heart stood great gates covered in unreadable symbols, guarded by spear-bearing soldiers.

The gates opened. Light poured through, harsh and bright.

They were brought to the Queen's throne room.

Queen 1—also called the Queen Mother, formally Her Majesty Queen the First, but most often simply *the Queen*—sat upon a throne of twisted resin and chitin, its surface glistening like amber in the dim light. She was massive, ancient, her carapace dulled to the colour of dried honey. Her wings hung in torn veils behind her, once splendid, now brittle. Antennae like cracked filigree quivered at every echo. A circlet of shed locust shells crowned her brow, and her many-faceted eyes burned with a weary amber light. Around her feet lay husks of attendants long gone, still bowing in eternal obeisance.

Her voice, when it came, was dry and full of dust, like paper rubbed against stone.

"Who is this?" she said, as if any interruption were an annoyance.

The commander bowed low. "Intruders. Captured at the north gate."

Tim stepped forward, fell to his knees, and held up the Zolodrev seed. "Your Majesty, we have stolen a Zolodrev seed to save our people and cure the ravening."

Viola stepped forward and showed the packets of Zolodrev fruit. "And food today—Zolodrev fruit, given by the worm-matriarchs themselves."

"We will see," the Queen said. She nodded to the commander, and he took the gifts and brought them to her. The fruit he placed beside her. The Zolodrev seed he handed to her. She held it, studying it.

Silence filled the hall. Only the Queen's eyes moved, scanning, suspicious.

"Lies," she said at last. "It's a trap."

Gasps rippled through the chamber.

"No—Your Majesty," Tim cried. "It's nourishment! The worms—"

"Worm deceit!" the Queen hissed. "They send you bearing death, and you call it mercy? I know their kind."

Viola tried to speak, but the Queen's wings shuddered, releasing a cloud of dust.

"Take them away," she said coldly. "And throw them in the dungeons before they spread more of their poison."

Guards seized them and hauled them through amber corridors that turned darker, deeper, colder.

They were thrown into a cell—walls of hardened resin, a single barred opening near the ceiling. The door slammed. A guard locked it.

Tim shouted through the door. "Fools!"

Pall helped Viola up.

Zazila and Zilili coiled together, shaking.

"So," Pall said quietly. "We've lost everything."

Viola pressed her hands against the amber wall. Solid. Unyielding. Beyond it, she could hear the hum of wings, the click of mandibles, the distant rage of a queen who no longer believed in hope.

"Yes," Viola answered. She turned to face her friends, small in the golden cell beneath the earth. "But we're not beaten. Not yet."

Chapter 35

Tim paced the amber floor, his boots clicking sharp and fast. "She's mad," he said at last. "Mad as a blind beetle in sunlight."

No one disagreed. The cell walls glowed faintly, trapping tired light. Beyond the barred doorway came the endless hum of wings.

"We can't reason with madness," Tim went on, his voice hardening. "And we don't need her permission. We'll go to Dampenia ourselves, plant the Zolodrev, and feed every starving locust in the realm." His antennae flattened. "Let the Queen rot in her amber tomb."

"Darling," said Zazila softly, "we're prisoners. And she took the seed."

"Then we fight our way out." Tim's claws flexed.

"Against trained soldiers?" Pall leaned against the wall, arms crossed.

Tim's mandibles clicked. "I'm not afraid to die."

"Well, I am." Pall looked up at the low ceiling. "But you're right that we have to get out. We're deep underground. This chamber's locust-sized—perfect for insects and worms. But what happens when the shrinking spell ends?"

Viola's head snapped up.

"We'd grow back to human size," Pall said. "In a space two inches high." He paused. "That would be… final."

Zilili's rings chimed nervously. "Well, you do get warning. Usually. An itchy feeling before —"

"Usually?" Pall interrupted.

"Probably," Zilili said, not meeting his eyes.

"Probably." Pall shut his eyes. "Wonderful."

Tim resumed pacing, faster now. "We came all this way. We survived Molgorod. We stole the seed." His voice cracked. "And for what? To be thrown in a dungeon by a queen who refuses to be saved?"

Viola had been staring at the amber wall, barely hearing them. In her mind she kept seeing the Queen's face — not the anger, not the madness, but what had flickered beneath.

Not hatred.

"She's not refusing to be saved," Viola said. "She's afraid."

They turned.

"What?" Tim asked.

"It wasn't for nothing." Viola's voice was quiet, but it carried in the small space. "And we're not giving up."

Tim's antennae lifted. "Viola —"

"We have to save her."

Tim's wings flared. "Save the queen who called our gifts poison? Who threw us in here?"

"Yes."

"But she's beyond help," Zazila cried. "Grief has broken her heart."

"Someone has to reach her," Viola said.

Zilili shook her head. "You can't mend a heart that old. That broken."

"We can try," said Viola.

"Why?" Pall asked — not arguing, only asking. "Why risk everything for someone who won't even look at hope when it's handed to her?"

Viola pressed her palm against the amber wall, feeling the faint warmth trapped within. She thought of Dampenia's people, who never tried.

The mermaid who'd given up her ring for lost. The blind walking trees, who only needed someone to stomp so they could find water. Even a Molgorodian who'd learned to sing. Every impossible thing they'd overcome had begun the same way — with someone too stubborn to accept that hope was dead.

"Because if the Queen has lost hope," Viola said quietly, "someone has to lend her theirs."

No one spoke. The resin walls hummed softly, as if the whole hive were holding its breath.

"How?" Pall asked at last.

Viola turned to face them. Her hands were trembling, but her voice was steady. "I don't know yet." She looked at each of them — Tim, antennae drooping with exhaustion; Pall, arms crossed against fear; Zazila and Zilili, wound together like a promise. "But I'm going to keep trying. Someone has to."

Tim was silent for a long moment. Then his antennae lifted slightly. "You're either the bravest person who ever lived," he said, "or the craziest."

"Maybe both," said Viola, and despite everything, she almost smiled.

The amber glow dimmed to dying gold. Beyond the walls came the sound of a thousand wings beating slowly, endlessly, waiting for something that would never come.

And somewhere above them, in her throne of twisted resin and grief, the Queen sat alone in her cathedral

of despair — too frightened to believe in seeds, or
fruit, or hope.

Chapter 36

The sound came first—a dry scrape of claws on resin. Then the door opened, flooding the cell with pale amber light.

"Prisoner," said a guard. "The Queen commands you."

"Which prisoner?" Tim demanded.

The guard pointed. "The crooked one."

Pall stiffened.

Viola stepped forward. "Wait—why him?"

The guard ignored her. "Bring the sword."

Pall glanced at Viola. She tried to look brave, though her mouth trembled.

"It'll be all right," he said, which sounded unconvincing even to him. Then he followed the guards out.

The corridors of amber were bright and silent, the air thick with the scent of dust and honey. When they reached the throne hall, the guards halted and pushed him forward alone.

Queen 1 sat motionless upon her glistening throne, eyes dull as old jewels.

She extended a claw. "The sword."

Pall held it out. "It's not really a sword," he said. "More of a—"

"Silence." She turned the weapon in her claws, studying its sheen. "Living wood of the elves."

"Yes," Pall said. "A gift."

"Unlikely." The Queen's antennae twitched. "No elf would gift such craft to a human. What is your true purpose? Speak the truth, and perhaps I will not kill you."

"I don't have a purpose," Pall said.

"Lies!" The word rang through the hall. "Why have you come?"

He hesitated. "I just… got caught up in Viola's adventure. Which I suppose is now mine too."

"So," the Queen said slowly, "she is your leader. I knew it. What is she plotting, sneaking through my kingdom?"

"She's not sneaking," Pall said quickly. "She's travelled across every land to find you."

The Queen leaned forward. "Then she is the killer, and you follow her orders."

"I'm not—she's not—"

"Who does she serve?" the Queen hissed. "Czar Vortan? King Uhm? Queen Isiiala? The brood-mother of the northern wyrms?"

"None of them," Pall said. "Viola's trying to save our people!"

"From what?"

He froze.

"From what?" the Queen repeated, her voice rising.

"From… the locusts," Pall said softly.

The Queen's wings flared. "I knew it! She seeks our destruction—as all humans do."

"No! That's not what I meant—"

"But she failed." The Queen rose to her full height, towering above him, her shadow cutting across the floor. "And for your honesty, I will not kill you."

From her abdomen she exuded a thick frothy foam that hissed as it met the air. Before Pall could move, it covered him— hot, clinging, hardening at once to amber shell. He tried to shout, but the

resin sealed his mouth; only his nose was left clear for breath.

The Queen examined the frozen figure before her. "You live," she said softly. "As I promised."

She turned the elven rapier once more, the living wood still faintly green in her claws. Then she placed it beside her throne like a trophy and called for the next prisoner.

Chapter 37

The sound of marching came again—closer this time, heavier. The guards filled the doorway, resin armour creaking.

"The Queen commands the locust," said the commander.

Tim's wings flared. "You're not taking me anywhere."

Viola stepped forward. "Where's Pall?"

No answer.

Tim lunged, striking one guard in the chest. The blow barely moved the insect, who struck back with the flat of his spear. Tim hit the wall and slid to the floor, dazed but still glaring.

Zilili began to hum a spell, her rings chiming. A guard turned and levelled his spear at her throat. "Try it," he said. "The Queen wants you alive, but not every part of you has to arrive."

Zazila hissed and coiled protectively around Tim. "You will not touch him."

"Stop!" Viola cried. "They're in love! Don't break them apart."

"A worm and a locust?" sneered one of the soldiers. "Disgusting."

Viola stared, appalled. "Love is never wrong," she said. "How can you say such a thing?"

The commander considered, then said flatly, "Bring the worm too. The Queen will decide what's wrong."

They seized them both. Tim struggled until two guards pinned him.

The cell door slammed, leaving Viola alone in the dim honey-light.

The throne hall glowed with dull amber fire. The Queen sat upon her resin seat, turning Pall's elven rapier in her claws. Nearby, the amber shell that held him upright caught the light and gleamed like a statue.

Tim stopped short when he saw it. "Pall…" he whispered.

"Silence," barked the commander. He bowed low. "Your Majesty—the prisoners, as ordered."

Zazila and Tim clung to each other. The Queen tilted her head, studying them. "A locust and a worm," she said softly. "Revolting."

Tim's temper flared. "How dare you—"

"Tim!" Zilili hissed, but too late.

The commander struck him across the back with his spear. "Show respect. That's your Queen."

Tim forced himself upright, breathing hard. "We came here to save you," he said. "And this is how you treat us?"

"You are a traitor and a spy," said the Queen.

"You are mad!"

The word rang through the hall. Every guard froze. Even the Queen was still.

When she spoke, her voice was cold as stone. "Commander. Bring him to me."

Zazila cried out, wrapping herself around Tim. "No!"

The guards dragged them apart. Tim fought, but it was no use. The guards were too strong.

Zilili held her sister.

Zazila wept.

The Queen rose, towering above them, sword in hand. The living wood shimmered faintly in the light. "Any last words, 93998544771114356?"

Zazila began to murmur something that sounded

like comfort, though in a tongue no one understood. No one paid attention.

Tim lifted his head. "My name is Tim."

The Queen swung the sword.

There was a flash of green light. Zilili shouted a word and vanished. In the same instant she and Zazila reappeared before Tim—shielding him from the blade.

The sword struck.

Zazila Zilili's body fell in two neat halves, her rings scattering across the resin floor like rain.

Tim dropped to his knees beside them. "No!" His cry echoed up the amber vaults and came back broken.

The Queen stood frozen, the rapier trembling in her claws. She looked down at the dead worm, then at the locust still kneeling, shaking with grief.

Her voice was quiet now, uncertain. "Get me the girl," she said.

Chapter 38

The itching began in her palms. Then her arms. Viola scratched without thinking, then froze.

"Oh no," she whispered.

Footsteps sounded in the corridor. The guards had come again.

"The Queen's command," said the commander.

Two locusts flanked her, spears low. She was marched through the amber halls—bright, echoing, filled with the hum of wings.

The throne chamber was worse than she'd imagined. Pall stood motionless inside a hardened shell of resin, his face dimly visible through amber glass. Nearby lay Tim, crumpled and breathing hard. And beside him—

Tim clutched the severed halves of Zazila Zilili, keening softly.

Viola's throat closed. "Oh no," she said. "Oh no, oh no."

The Queen turned her heavy head. "Come here, girl."

Viola stepped forward, trembling. "Your Majesty… what have you done?"

The Queen's tone was almost bored. "I didn't intend to kill her. She teleported into the blade. It isn't my fault if she wished to die for a locust."

"But *why?*" Viola's voice cracked.

"You can stop pretending." The Queen's claws tightened on the arms of her throne. "I know you've come to kill me. Your warrior confessed everything."

"He *what?* No—I don't want to kill anyone."

"Many have tried, you know." The Queen's voice was flat, as if reciting something memorized long ago.

"Your Majesty, I mean you no harm."

The Queen gave a dry, rattling laugh. "My dear, you're not in a position to harm anyone."

"Actually," said Viola quietly, "that might not be true."

The Queen's antennae flicked forward. "Explain."

"The worms gave us a potion to shrink, so we could reach you safely. But it wears off." Viola held up her hands. They were trembling—and red with scratching. "When it does, we'll grow again. Large enough to break through these tunnels. To collapse the hive. To hurt everyone."

"More lies," the Queen snapped. But her voice wavered. Her gaze dropped to Viola's hands.

"Zilili said we'd feel itchy before it happened," Viola said. "And a few minutes ago, I started to feel it."

The Queen went very still. "When I cut her down."

"Maybe?"

"Of course." The Queen's laugh was bitter. "The worms would ensure their own safety—or my death. Clever."

From the floor, Tim stirred. His voice came out raw with grief. "You're a monster."

"No, Tim," Viola said gently. "She's not."

The Queen's head snapped toward her. "What?"

"She's good and kind."

The Queen barked a harsh, broken laugh. "What trick is this?"

"No trick. Your Majesty—you're strong, and brave, and good. I know you are. You tried to save your people. You went to the Czar's garden for the Zolodrev fruit."

Something flickered across the Queen's face— something old and wounded. Her voice dropped. "I was a fool."

"No," Viola said. "What the Czar did was wrong. What *you* did was right. You found the way to save your people." She glanced at Tim. "The ravening is terrible. My friend will be overcome by it in less than a year. I don't want that for him. Or for anyone."

For a moment—just a heartbeat—the Queen's expression softened. Her claw moved, almost unconsciously, toward the wrapped bundle near her throne.

Then her face hardened again. She pulled her claw back. "I will not be fooled twice. You work for Vortan. Only he knew I begged him to share his fruit. Only he knew he refused—and ordered my people destroyed."

"Your Majesty," Viola said, her voice steady despite the itching spreading up her arms, "you don't have to believe me. The fruit is right there. If you taste it, you'll see there's still reason to hope."

"We both know it's poison."

"Then let me eat it," Viola said. "Or Tim. Or your commander. Anyone. *Please.*"

The Queen stared at her. At the fruit. Back at her.

"Who do you serve?" she asked.

Viola took a breath. "I don't think you understand. I don't serve anyone. I'm just a girl. An ordinary girl."

"An ordinary girl," the Queen repeated slowly. "Wearing elven cloth. Carrying tales of seeds and miracles."

"Yes." Viola paused, searching for words. "I'm not a hero. I'm just… The people of Dampenia—my people—we live in rain. Bad things happen, and mostly we accept them. That's just how it is. But then the Brean came, starving, and we shared what we had. They ate every pricklepepper in the kingdom until only one was left. My mother said, 'Well, that's that.' But I thought—no. Someone has to try."

She met the Queen's eyes. "So I started walking. And I met people. The merfolk. The elves. The moles. The worms. And I just kept hoping. That's all I've ever done."

The hall was silent except for Tim's quiet weeping.

The Queen stared at Viola for a long moment. When she spoke, her voice was barely a whisper. "I cannot hope. Hope is gone for me."

"You don't have to hope," Viola said softly. "You just have to let me hope for you."

Silence.

The Queen's claw trembled. Slowly—so slowly—she reached toward the wrapped bundle. Her movements were stiff, mechanical, as if forcing herself through water.

She lifted the fruit.

Set it on the table before her.

Her claws fumbled with the waxed leaves. The wrapping fell away. The scent of summer filled the air—honey and sunlight and growing things.

The Queen stared at the fruit. Her antennae quivered. "If this is poison…"

"It isn't," Viola whispered.

The Queen's claw closed around the fruit. She raised it. Hesitated. Her whole body shook.

Then she bit down.

Snap.

The sound echoed through the hall.

The Queen froze, the fruit still pressed to her mandibles.

Pop.

Her eyes widened.

Snap-pop.

A flush began at her mandibles—a wave of gold spreading across her carapace like sunrise breaking over still water. The dull amber of her shell deepened to honey. To light. Her torn wings shivered and straightened, catching the glow.

"I…" The Queen's voice cracked. She stared at the fruit in her claws as if seeing it for the first time. "I can't…"

She took another bite.

Snap-pop-snap-pop.

Colour flooded through her. The grey film over her eyes cleared. Her antennae lifted, trembling, sensing the air as if she'd been deaf and suddenly heard music.

"It's real," she whispered. Then louder, wonder breaking through her voice like light through clouds: "It… it *is* Zolodrev fruit!"

A sound rose in the hall—soft at first, then swelling. The guards' wings began to hum. Not the dull, endless drone of despair, but something higher. Brighter.

The hive was singing.

The Queen looked down at Viola. Tears—actual tears—gleamed in her compound eyes. "Child," she said, and her voice was young again, trembling with something that had been buried for years. "What have you done?"

"Nothing," Viola said, and she was crying too. "I just hoped."

The Queen set down the fruit. Her claws shook as she covered her face. Her shoulders heaved once. Twice.

Then she stood—taller than before, stronger—and her voice rang clear through the chamber:

"Release the prisoners. All of them. *Now.*"

The guards scrambled to obey. Two rushed to Pall, already working to crack the amber shell. Others lifted Tim gently, carefully.

But the Queen's eyes stayed on Viola. "I have been so afraid," she said quietly. "For so long."

"I know," Viola said.

The Queen bent down—an ancient, terrible, beautiful creature—and touched her claw to Viola's cheek. "Thank you," she whispered, "for being braver than I was."

Behind them, amber cracked. Pall gasped and stumbled free, alive.

The hive hummed louder.

And somewhere in the walls, in the honeycombed chambers and endless corridors, ten thousand locusts felt it—felt their queen return to herself, felt hope kindle like a flame passed from hand to hand to wing.

Chapter 39

all broke free of the resin with a sound like cracking sugar.

"Viola, we have to go."

She was kneeling by her pack, rummaging frantically. "Where is it—where is it?"

"What are you doing?"

"The itching's getting worse," she said through her teeth. "We've got to get out before—before we burst. But I need the elf-water. We might still help Zazila and Zilili."

Tim darted across the amber floor, wings trembling. "I'll find it! I'll use it like we did with Fang—just go!"

"Don't give up!" Viola called, even as Pall seized her hand and pulled her to her feet.

Together they ran through the echoing corridors, past the stunned guards, the itch rising to a fever beneath their skin.

By the time they reached the great bridge, their limbs had begun to change. Pall's arms lengthened until his knuckles brushed the floor. Viola's ears stretched, her left foot ballooned, her right hand puffed like a loaf of bread.

"Keep running!" she gasped.

They lumbered across the bridge as their bodies swelled, each step shaking the resin span. Locust warriors dove for cover as the pair grew larger and larger. Then—at the far side, in the mouth of the Barrowmere tunnel—they popped back to full size in a sudden, breathless instant.

Pall's back scraped the ceiling; dust rained down. Viola fell laughing against the wall.

"Alive," she panted.

He grinned. "Barely. I hope Zazila and Zilili were saved."

Inside the castle, something stranger still was happening.

Tim had found the vial of elf-water and poured it over the two severed worm halves, pressing the pieces together as if willing life back into them. The water hissed faintly, blue against the amber light.

At first, nothing. Then both bodies twitched. The cut edges rippled and—against all sense—new flesh began to bud and knit, pushing the two halves apart and forming mirror halves where none had been.

"Extraordinary," murmured the Queen, pausing in her slow chewing of the Zolodrev fruit. "I did not expect *that*."

The halves writhed and lengthened. Within minutes two complete worms lay coiled where one body had been. The air smelled faintly of sap and magic.

Zazila wiggled. "I'm alive?"

Zilili wriggled. "So am I."

Below them, two new wormlets stirred—their newly grown halves, bright and small as polished roots. One lifted her soft head. "Are you my mummy?"

"I suppose I am," said Zazila, dazed.

The other new half blinked up at Zilili. "Can we do magic too?"

Zilili smiled, proud despite the chaos. "With practice."

Soon the four of them were wriggling in delighted confusion, chattering about names and spells and snack times. The elder pair decided their new halves were daughters, not copies.

The Queen began distributing the remaining Zolodrev fruit among her court. All across the resin halls came the sound of popping and snapping as the locusts tasted the fruit, their hunger vanishing.

Tim watched Zazila and Zilili with their tiny daughters, his relief edged with confusion. Am I still engaged? he wondered.

Zazila reached toward him. "Aren't you going to say hello to your daughter?"

"Um… hello?" he said.

The wormlet happily wiggled against him. "Daddy!"

Zilili slithered over and gently rubbed Zazila's wormlet. Then she turned to Tim. "You are a very fine locust, Tim, but I am not in love with you. I don't know if I ever will be."

Zazila beamed. "How splendid! Then we needn't fight about it."

Her sister nodded. "If you wish to marry my other half, you have my approval."

Tim bowed, relieved and flustered.

The Queen lifted her goblet and declared, "A wedding, then! I shall marry them myself!"

Chapter 40

he wedding was short but beautiful. At Tim's insistence, they held it on the resin bridge so that Pall and Viola—now regrown to human size—could attend.

Through some miracle of worm magic, they still understood Insect Common, and the Queen herself performed the ceremony in that tongue.

Zazila wore a wreath of silk-grass, hastily woven by spiders who had heard the news and wished to help. Tim stood beside her, his wings brushed clean of dust, trying not to vibrate with nerves. Zilili gave her sister away. The commander stood in for Tim's family. All Brean were kin, having all been birthed by the Queen—so he counted.

"We are gathered," said the Queen, "in the deep places of the earth, where love has been rare and light rarer still. But today we remember that even in darkness, two souls may find each other.

"Do you, Timothy 93998544771114356, called Tim, promise to cherish this worm, to face the ravening together, and to build a life worth living?"

"I do," said Tim, his voice steady.

"And do you, Zazila of Zuzzuz, promise the same?"

"I do!" she cried. Her wormlet cried too, though she did not understand what was happening—only that her mother was happy.

"Then by the power vested in me by sorrow, survival, and hope reborn," said the Queen, "I declare you married. May your life together be sweeter than Zolodrev fruit."

The hall erupted in wing-song—deafening, joyful, alive. Tim and Zazila touched foreheads, the closest a locust and a worm could come to a kiss, while the new daughters cheered in high, piping voices.

Viola applauded until her hands hurt. Pall let out a small cheer, his earlier melancholy forgotten. Even Zilili swayed with happiness.

As the celebration began—locusts carrying out jars of fungus-wine and crystallized honey—the Queen approached Viola.

"Thank you," she said quietly.

"For what?"

"For not giving up on me, even when I gave you every reason to." Her voice dropped. "I nearly killed you all.

I nearly destroyed the last hope my people had. And still you stood there telling me I was good."

"You are good," Viola said. "You just forgot for a while."

The Queen's antennae trembled. "I have been afraid for so long, I forgot what else I could be."

"You're remembering now," said Viola. "That's what matters."

The Queen nodded slowly. Then she straightened, regal once more. "Tomorrow we plant the seed. But tonight"—she gestured to the celebration—"tonight we remember how to hope."

Music rose. Tim danced awkwardly with his new wife while Zazila cradled her sleeping daughter.

Pall finally allowed himself to smile.

Viola felt something settle in her chest. They had done it—the impossible thing, again. But she was tired, bone-tired, and homesick for rain, pricklepeppers, and her mother's exasperated sighs.

"One more ceremony," she whispered. "Then we can go home."

Pall heard. "Tomorrow," he said. "We'll plant the tree, and then we'll find our way back to Dampenia."

"Together?"

"Obviously together." He bumped her shoulder. "Someone has to make sure you don't adopt any more impossible quests on the way."

She laughed—really laughed—for the first time in days.

She pulled off Fang's whistle and tied it on a

string around her neck. "Do you think he'll bite us if I use it?"

"You want me to ride him again?!"

"Fastest way home short of flying. And we're too big to fly now," she said with a smile.

"Why did I ever follow you?" he moaned.

But then she kissed him on the cheek, and he stopped complaining.

Around them, the hive sang. And deep in the earth, in the Queen's chamber, the Zolodrev seed waited in its silk wrapping—ready to become something miraculous.

Chapter 41

iola and Pall stood at the mouth of the Barrowmere burrow. The northern wind pressed against them, flinging rain in silver slants across the hills. Viola raised her patchwork umbrella and listened to its hopeful tune—the soft drumming of drops above, the trickle of water sliding down the slope below.

Before them, the hillside swarmed with life. Word had spread through the secret channels of the earth— through tunnels, vibrations, and scent—that the Brean Queen had been saved, and that a Zolodrev seed was to be planted. Thousands of locusts stood assembled.

Other creatures had come too. Rhinoceros beetles had given off racing for the day and stood gleaming like iron kettles, their horns polished for the occasion. Ladybugs clustered in merry circles, singing bright songs and drumming cheerful rhythms on their crimson armour. Ants marched in perfect lines, each bearing a dewdrop as tribute. A delegation of mantises stood motionless in what might have been reverence—or judgment. Even the night-moths had gathered, their powdery wings fluttering like silent applause.

Behind them, the Talpan had crept partway from their tunnels—Humhum, Numni, and a score of others—stooping shyly at the edge of the rain. They did not like the light, but they understood ceremony.

Then the Queen emerged.

She rode upon a great stag beetle, its polished shell reflecting the rain like beaten metal, its horn curved upward in stately pride. Upon her brow rested a crown of woven antennae and chitin. Behind her came Tim, small yet radiant, carrying the Zolodrev seed wrapped in silk thread. And behind him glided Zazila and Zilili, twin arcs of gleaming rings and composure. Their new daughters, bright and half-grown, swivelled their heads from side to side, marvelling at the rain.

The Queen halted before a shallow pit ringed with fresh soil. The locust workers had dug it through the night and lined it with powdered leaf and sap.

Tim stepped forward with the seed, Zilili beside him. At a nod from the Queen, he turned to the waiting multitude.

"My people," he began, his voice carrying surprisingly far, "we have eaten much, fought much, and feared much. But there is one thing we have never tried in all our long buzzing: to grow. This seed was bought with courage from every kind of creature—mole, worm, bird, and child. Let it remind us that plenty is not stolen but shared. Let us become a swarm that feeds the world."

He knelt and set the Zolodrev seed into the earth.

Zilili raised her rings, murmured the ancient words, and touched the soil. A faint golden glow pulsed outward. The ground trembled. From the hole rose a pale tendril, then another, curling toward the rain. The hill erupted in a roar of wings and voices.

"Grow!" shouted the Brean. "Grow!"

The Queen dismounted and crossed to Pall. Her voice, when she spoke, was clear and dry as paper.

"You are not of my kind, but you stood beside those who were. You carried loyalty through fear, which is rarer than strength. Know that the Brean remember you, knight of the rain."

Pall bowed awkwardly, rain dripping from his hair.

Then the Queen turned to Viola. "And you," she said, "whose hope is louder than reason. You gave faith to those who had forgotten the word. When this tree bears its first fruit, a seed shall be sent across the

world to Dampenia. Let it grow there as a reminder—
that even in the wettest, weariest kingdom, something
golden may rise."

Viola tried to answer but found her throat tight. She
only nodded.

Above them, the young Zolodrev shivered in the
wind. Its leaves unfolded like small hands catching the
rain, and the rain kept falling—patient and endless—
as if the sky itself waited to see what would grow.

Author's Note

When my children were small, we used to play a game called *And Then What Happened?* One of us would begin a story, the next would carry it on, and the next would change it entirely. A knight might become a cook, a cook might become a unicorn, and the unicorn might float away as a balloon. Logic did not always attend. But the stories were alive, which seemed the important thing.

Halfway through *Viola the Great*, I realized I was playing that game. Strange and marvellous things kept happening to Viola. She never set out to be great or brave; she simply noticed that no one else was doing anything, and decided she might as well. Pall is the same sort—tired, kind, and determined despite himself. Between them, they muddle through miracles.

I like stories where the magic is unexpected. Where the world can be a little frightening, yet full of decency if you look. You don't need to be splendid to be good. You only need to keep trying. If the world sometimes feels too big or peculiar, remember Viola. Hold up your umbrella, take a step, and see what happens next. That's how every story worth telling goes on.

If you are interested in finding out more about me and my novels, please visit www.harwoodjones.com and leave a comment. I'd love to hear from you.

—Troy